VOLUME ONE

NAYLOR'S WAR

By R Poyton

THIS IS AN INNSMOUTH GOLD BOOK

ISBN: 978-0-9956454-9-3   Paperback

Cover design: Innsmouth Gold

Published by Innsmouth Gold.

www.innsmouthgold.com

Dedicated to
Sky Warriors everywhere

CHAPTER 1

READY FOR ANYTHING

Dropping onto a planet's surface from a couple of klicks up is a never less than exhilarating experience. First, there is the long wait in a cramped pod as the Fat Albert gets into position. Some say that the waiting is the worst part. They are wrong. The worst part is when the bay door slides silently away from under your feet to reveal the surface far, far below.

Then comes the exquisite moment when a puff of compressed air blasts you out into space. From that gentle puff, you hit the slipstream of a vessel travelling at around 500kph. The first thing you do is spin, the second is scream. Space, surface and sky jumble in a trio of desperate tumbling until your suit gyros kick in. From there, it's simply a matter of falling fifteen hundred metres while your view quickly changes from continent to country, to province, to district, to battle zone to patch of dirt with your name on it.

Not that you have time to take in the view because your suit is talking to you, see? Your HUD is flashing up your height, wind speed, air speed, angle, trajectory, coordinates and seconds in luminous green numbers. It even has my name and number displayed, NAYLOR, M. B57861773.

Meanwhile, in your earpiece a computerised voice is running through your Equipment Roster Check and Mission Outline. Added to that, every ten seconds you get another voice constantly repeating your Status Code, which ranges from *A* for Free Fall through to *C* for Combat Ready to *G* for Medical Emergency. I've never heard the SC for Dead, I presume it is *H*. Why you'd need to be told you are dead, I don't know, but the army is nothing if not thorough.

Some say the purpose of the ERC and MO is to take your mind off the fact that you are a single individual free falling from a couple of klicks up towards a hard, rocky surface. If so, it doesn't work. Some things are primal. No one ever leapt to his death calmly reciting a shopping list. Most of us scream at some point, if not out loud then internally. Don't believe the recruitment films, they never show the best bits. Landers in those have a steely eye and a square jaw and never piss their pants on the way down.

So, there you are, a small speck in the sky rapidly

growing larger. If all is well, your retros will have fired by now and your descent becomes a more measured affair. If not, enjoy the last ninety seconds of your life. At this stage you can almost begin to relax, look around and admire the view. Of course, the view is a battlefield which kicks the adrenaline back in but, hey, this is what you signed up for, right? And now it is happening, spread out beneath you in a glorious panorama. The flash of tracer, the columns of black smoke, the crump of explosions and the rending of metal. Then you hear human voices as your suit drops into range of the surface unit comsnet.

If you are lucky, the enemy on the ground will be too busy to look up and you hit dirt as planned – right place, right time, right equipment. But this is the army after all, so two out of three is a good day. Which is what I'm having right now. Right place, right time but there's a red light flashing on my HUD which I'm none too happy about. One retro is firing sporadically and according to my ERC, I'm light on ammo. Only the army could spend untold thousands of credits to train a man, fly him vast distances in a huge space-ship to drop him on a planet in a state of the art exosuit, then allocate him only two mags of ammo. Still, it's better that particular leg of the stool is wonky rather than the other two. No one likes being dropped into a ravine, ocean or active volcano.

At a hundred metres up, things below start making

sense, the training kicks in and you begin planning. Troop positions become clear, fire zones take shape and areas of cover become apparent. If all is going to plan, you become aware of your squad members around you. There's a feeling of safety in numbers, even if it's selfishly because you are no longer a lone target. The last fifty metres is the quickest and the landing always takes me by surprise, even with the in-ear countdown. Terra firma underfoot kills off the last vestiges of any nerves and once again you are a soldier, not a helpless target in free fall.

I hit the ground hard, thanks to the misfiring retro. A sharp jolt but nothing breaks. Immediately it's time for RCO – Roll, Cover, Orientate. On their first jump, most Landers simply lie there motionless on landing, in relief at having hit dirt. In action, that makes you a nice target. So I impact, immediately hunker down and roll into nearby cover; in this case behind a half submerged concrete pipe. Zoning out the HUD, I scan my immediate surroundings while the suit clicks and whirs and automatically deploys my side arm and ammo. The outer heat shields fall away, along with the Exo head set and I'm left fully armed in a standard GAS. I patch into the squad comsnet and report.

"Angel one seven, ground, Status C".

That means Combat Ready, remember? C for Combat, I guess; the army never over-estimates the intelligence of us Landers. I feel and hear the rest of the platoon forming up around me. There's a tap on my shoulder as Bradshaw crouches by my side. Captain Sangha's voice crackles over the net.

"Team Beta, advance to Position Four, attack formation!"

That means pyramid formation, groups of three, heavy weapons on the flanks, Command Team in the centre. Kaur has moved quietly between Bradshaw and myself and grins at us both. Before we move off I ask if they can spare me a mag each, as my supply is low. They oblige, it's what friends are for. One final check and we move off in a low crouch. At this stage there is no welcome from the other chap - he is fully engaged with our ground units. It gives the squad a chance to form up , though I notice one figure is missing. Kaur sees my glance and shakes her head.

"Joubert piled in. Suit malfunction."

Shit. His first combat op. But no time for that now, we get into position, release safeties and advance. Basic training kicks in and the unit swings into action.

CHAPTER 2

BASIC TRAINING

Basic training, two words. Basic, as in easy to grasp, fundamental. And training, to be taught how to do something. A simple phrase, easy to understand. But oh, what a world of suffering they conceal! I was like most soldiers, I suppose, just seventeen when I signed up. Prior to that, a life of petty crime and casual violence, kicked out of school, my poor Ma at her wit's end. Prospects looked limited.

It was at a local civic function that I saw a display of unarmed combat from Landers 3, part of a combined services display that was touring the Home Systems. I thought the stuff looked good but too fancy for real life. I didn't hesitate to tell the Corporal so, too. I was a mouthy kid back in the day and far too sure of myself. He smiled, of course, and invited me onto the mats. Well, I had my mates with me, there was no backing down. It was the first painful lesson of many. I had enthusiasm and some strength but no method. Still, I got up twice before he knocked me spark out on the third go. When I came round, my friends had left and the Corporal was holding a cold towel to my head.

"You'll be alright, lad," he told me. "I just gave you a wee clip, that's all."

So from there we got talking. He admired my guts, I admired his skills. He showed me what he'd done and explained how the demo stuff was strictly that, a showy demo for public consumption. Real combat, he assured me, was a different beast entirely. Something about his quiet confidence stirred an interest in me. I'd never thought of joining the military before. Still, if I signed up now, it was only for Basic Training. Twenty eight weeks away from this shit hole.

Life on Slipher 5 didn't have much going for it, apart from it's Earth-like conditions. It had been established as a mining colony about sixty years back, though half the mines had been closed when I was a kid. Hence the local propensity for crime, moonshine and violence. Most of us ended up working in factories, which involved not much more than turning up and pulling levers for an eight hour shift. Local entertainment consisted of bars and dives, none of which you'd take your mother to. A certain level of drug use was tolerated by the authorities and life beyond school promised little more than days grinding into weeks, grinding into months and years. I had nothing to look forward to except more crime, drink and prison, like the old man, I reckoned. If I didn't like the army training, I'd just do a bunk. So I took all the info, went home and told Ma, then, next day, went off to the local recruiting office.

The place was a store front for all the services and the first thing they told me was that I couldn't just sign up to the Landers like that. First, I had to put time in with a regular unit. A couple of years there then I could apply for selection. The guy behind the desk said I probably shouldn't bother though, I'd be far better off sticking with the regulars. They would teach me a trade, he said, I could come out qualified in tech, coms, engineering, catering, or one of half a dozen other vocations. Catering? To me that sounded like going back to school, with added army bullshit on top.

So I nodded politely and said thanks but the Landers was my goal. The signing officer shook his head and laughed, like he had some private joke, but he put the papers through anyway. Looking back, I was lucky to get in at all. Pre-rebellion, the services were being run down and their budgets cut back. Most army work back then involved close protection for our glorious leaders, security at key installations and the occasional scuffle with smugglers or gangsters - that was usually a joint-op with the Navy. Anyway, I had an interview and a medical and not long after my E-papers came through.

A week later, I was sat in the back of a General Transport Vehicle with an old suitcase and fifteen other bods heading for the local shuttle base. I recognised a couple of the others as well known herberts and we nodded guardedly to each other. From the base we were lifted up into low orbit and placed on a Navy transport, which then made a jump through our SysGate and deposited us on Krasinsky 3, home of ITC Delta. That's where my real experience began.

The greeting was friendly enough. The Corporal was quite civil to us as he showed us our quarters and explained how to stow what little gear we had. Packed away, we were shown to the canteen and given a hot meal. You could see where the money wasn't being spent, the food was more a case of *try and eat it* than *come and get it*. Still, it filled the belly. That done, it was back to barracks where we changed into green boiler suits. We would get our uniforms the next day, the Corp told us.

"Oh," he added laughing, before switching the light off and leaving the room, "and tomorrow you'll also meet

CSM Holland."

And meet him we did, first thing the next morning. When I say morning I really mean night time. Well, that's what I call 0400. The army obviously has a different view.

Deep in snooze-land the twenty of us, when the lights go on, an alarm blares out over and over and above it all the sweet, dulcet tones of the CSM, screaming at us to get up. So get up we did and were ordered to attention at the foot of our beds. Now Holland was real old school. Not a tall man but incredibly broad shouldered, his uniform immaculate. When he got annoyed, you could see a vein throbbing in his temple. It was throbbing most of the time. Up and dressed, he double-timed us out to the parade ground where we stood shivering in the early morning air. Stood in four ragged rows, Holland took up position in front of us at ramrod attention and, with a voice like a megaphone, roared at us.

"Attention! Shoulders back, eyes front! Hands at sides, stand up straight there!" There was a shifting in the ranks and a general stiffening of posture. The CSM glared at us, then continued.

"My name is Company Sergeant Major N Holland. Does anyone know what the N stands for?"

A few of us looked at each other uncertainly. None dare speak except for one bright spark whose voice floated over from the rear rank.

"Is it Nimrod, sir?"

A titter rippled through the lines and Holland's vein began throbbing.

"No, it is not! The N stands for Nightmare. And it is I who has the unfortunate and unappetising task of attempting to turn you sorry sacks of shit into something resembling soldiers! Now drop, fifty press ups!"

I grunted to the bod next to me "I think I prefer Nimrod," as we began the first of the endless round of exercises.

My personal introduction to the CSM came as he stood right behind me. And I mean right behind, I could feel his breath on my neck and smell his cheap aftershave. He whispered, mouth close to my ear.

"Am I hurting you hair, son?"

Confused by this odd question, I answered "No, Sergeant."

His response, without moving position, was to scream at full volume.

"Well I should be, I'm bleeding well standing on it! Get it cut!"

Then he was off down the line to berate the next poor sod. Duly exercised and inspected, we got our first glimpse of a real life officer. He even had a little box to stand on. Our group had been joined by several others, so there were now around sixty of us lined up in the cold. The officer took the podium and, in a clear nasal voice, introduced himself as Lieutenant Rawalpindi.

"Welcome to ITC Delta. You are all here as volunteers for our wonderful armed forces. This is a great opportunity, both for you to help defend our beloved Alliance and also to develop yourself fully as soldiers. I'm sure a glorious future awaits you!"

"Or a bone sack in an unmarked grave," muttered the guy next to me.

"We now come to an important event," the Lieutenant continued, in a voice full of importance. "You are to be sworn in. This sacred oath binds you to service in the Alliance for as long as your period of service lasts. Furthermore, on being discharged, the Alliance reserves the right to call you back into duty should the need arise. Now, raise you right hands and repeat after me. I, insert name here, do solemnly swear..."

The inevitable happened, almost to a man the unit repeated, "I, insert name here, do solemnly swear..."

I thought Holland was going to have a cardiac arrest. Rawalpindi sneered from his podium then addressed Holland.

"Sergeant Major, these men appear to believe they are on a day trip. Please apprise these... people... of the fact that there is no place for levity here. I will return in an hour when we shall administer the oath. Properly."

With that, he strode off and the CSM positively growled with delight before screaming us up and down that parade ground until every recruit was a wheezing wreck. Suitably chastised, we each echoed Rawalpindi's words properly on his return. Apparently satisfied, he turned to the CSM again.

"Much better, Sergeant Major. Now, get these men outfitted, jabbed and fed. I'll inspect them in a week's time."

Then he strode off again and the group was lined up and fed into the army's processing machine.

First step was to be sat in a chair while a bored looking barber shaved your head virtually bald. It was quite an odd thing, catching a glimpse of yourself in the mirror after. I'd always worn my hair quite long so it was a bit of shock looking up and seeing the new me staring back. I'd always been quite tall and lean but I figured this new look suited me just fine. I reckoned myself a bit of a tough guy. That particular bubble was soon burst.

From there we were issued with uniforms. Cheap material from the looks of it, and no doubt tight where they should be loose and loose where they should be tight. Alongside the uniform each of us received a dog-tag, *to be removed only in the event of death* the graven face store man informed each of us with a cheerless grin.

Of course this being the army, we were not to put on our uniforms yet, there was one final humiliation. Each of us stripped naked and, carrying our uniforms in a neatly folded pile, were lined up for *jabs*. This, I found out, was a series of injections against various types of nasty that could be encountered while out on active service.

The queue ran ahead and into an open doorway, out from which issued the occasional cry of pain and swearing. Once in, you ran a gauntlet of white-coated types who punched a syringe in your arm as you passed. Fainting, which some did, was no defence, they simply got jabbed on the floor then dragged out by the ankles. That done, barely able to lift our arms, we were finally allowed to put on our uniforms and get some grub from the canteen.

This was just the start, of course. The 0400 wake up became a regular feature for our first week. Any infraction meant press ups, a run, or usually both. On one occasion, we were hosed down with cold water in the square after one unfortunate was found to have wet the bed. We had a week of this, Rawalpindi returning, as promised, for our first inspection. We failed, of course, I was beginning to get an idea of how this thing worked.

I was disappointed, though, that so far there'd been no sign of fight training or cool weaponry. Being the big mouth I was, I raised it with the CSM one day. I thought he was going to burst, that vein was pulsing so much.

"Let me explain!" he shouted in my face. "Guns is for men! You are not men! You are maggots! What are you?"

"Maggots, Sergeant," we dutifully replied.

"Exactly! So drop down on the floor and crawl, maggots! Five times round the square!"

Well it made a change from running. I never did ask again but, to be fair I began to see over the weeks how the CSM's training was preparing us. Those left in the group - ten had already dropped out - began losing surplus padding and filling out the shoulders of our uniforms. We began bonding as a team, even if it was just in hatred of the CSM. We became determined that he would never catch us out in inspections, and soon everything was spotless and in its rightful place.

To his credit, he actually began dropping compliments too, small ones but when he muttered to you "Good lad." you knew it meant something.

Six weeks in, we got our first guns. I use the term "guns" advisedly, they were more antique than gun but they did at least go bang and fire bullets. Having learnt my lesson, I let someone else ask the stupid question.

"Why don't we get proper guns, Sergeant?"

The CSM rolled his eyes as if talking to idiots.

"Because, Mr Clever Dick, giving you a proper gun

would be like giving a monkey a chainsaw. It wouldn't know what to do with it and would end up killing half its own group."

I took monkeys as being a step up the ladder from maggots. In any case, I enjoyed firing the old guns, they gave a satisfying kick in the shoulder and the wood smelt nice and felt good to the touch. The Range Instructor gave us another good reason for learning the old-fashioned way, too. Hi-tec was all well and good, he said but never rely on it. It's the man that counts at the end of the day and technology will always let you down at some point. He was right, of course but I wasn't going to find that out until much later.

The hand to hand training was much more disappointing, nothing like that Lander Corp had shown me. All we got was a couple of hours of very basic stuff. Fortunately, there were people on the base running various martial arts classes, which I trained in whenever I could, picking up some extra skills here and there.

Anyway, I got through Basic and was shipped out to a unit involved in security duties, mostly guarding military bases, government offices and the like. A few months in, just as I was about to die of boredom, the unit transferred out to the Rim. This was pre-rebellion days but it was already a wild place and I started getting my first taste of actual operations.

Smuggling was a huge problem. Cuts to the Navy meant they had to reduce patrols so there was no way they could cover all the main routes. That meant a change in strategy. Rather than attempting to intercept smuggler ships, it was decided instead that the PBI would carry out raids on the criminals' bases and installations.

It was also the time of the first riots; looking back, a precursor to the rebellion itself. Food shortages and political unrest led to sporadic outbreaks of violence in many of the Rim colonies. Units like ours were sent in to bolster the local police presence, not work that I found much to my liking. Too many of the people I was up against were just like the kids back home. Still, the higher ups insisted we crack down hard and crack down hard we did. Turned out we were pouring petrol on a fire. Anyway, a couple of tours in and I earned my first stripes. In reality I was ticking the days off until I could apply for the Landers.

Every cloud has a silver lining. When the Spart rebellion kicked off proper, diplomacy wasn't getting anywhere. Things were rapidly going pear shaped, so there was a move to expand the forces. That was my cue to apply for selection, though my a-hole of a CO made me jump through hoops. By then, I was stationed back in the Home Systems; there was no real action or danger there.

The rebellion proper started, I believe, with some dispute about mineral rights on a shitty little asteroid. No one could have predicted how it would spread; from a handful of miners on a small asteroid, to the whole of the frontier colonies. It gathered ground as it went until it was virtually a full-blown civil war. Still, like I said, I put my request in then sat and waited for a few weeks while the gears slowly ground. Typical army, when it's you who wants something, they move like treacle.

CHAPTER 3

SELECTION

I've removed my suit helmet, placed my red beret on my head at the required non-regulation angle and am taking a drag from my syg when Kaur saunters over. The position has been taken and the Engineers are now moving up to crack the few remaining bunkers ahead. I nod to her and smile as she raises her eyebrows at my flagrant lack of SOP. Helmets are supposed to stay on at all times in the battle zone, even one that has recently been cleared. You never know who might still be lurking amongst the wreckage waiting to take a pop, I suppose. But balls to that, I needed a smoke.

"Report?" I ask her.

"Objectives achieved, no enemy survivors. Our only loss was Joubert."

"Poor sod. Report the suit malfunction to the Brass but notify his family that he was killed in action. It will be bad enough for them as it is, without knowing he was killed by shoddy equipment."

"Will do, Sarge. Hey, you shouldn't smoke those

things, you know they will kill you."

She smiled and turned away to carry out the rest of her duties.

Kaur was a good soldier. I first met her during Selection. Once my paperwork came through, I was shipped out to a transport hub and from there on to Lander Base Alpha at Veytis 2. This was the real deal, the off-world HQ of the regiment. There was a lot of history here, much of it on display in the form of holopics in the main entrance hallway. The Landers pride themselves in following the traditions of the Airborne units of old. In some cases there are direct links, families who have served over the generations. Being a Sky Warrior is in the blood, it seems, we are born not made according to some.

I don't know about that but I do know that Landers consider themselves part of a special family, one that you are in for life whether you are still on service or not. The uniform might go but no Lander ever gets rid of his red beret. I had no concept yet of just how difficult it was going to be to get one. I thought Basic had been tough, it was nothing but an appetiser for what awaited us at LBA.

My batch consisted of thirty-two fellow recruits. At our Induction meeting we were told by the Corporal that what faced us was three months intense work, starting with a review of the Basics and culminating in Final

Selection. He stressed that it was not enough to be adequate at anything, we had to be *shit hot*. If it got too much, any recruit could ask to be Returned To Unit, RTU'd, at any time.

The Corporal also informed us that our time here would be light on the typical army bull, we were to take responsibility for our own kit and appearance, there would be no inspections. Personally, I didn't believe him; I thought it was a trick to catch us out. I couldn't imagine any army trainer missing out on the opportunity of an inspection. In any case, the Corporal stressed it would be hard, physically and emotionally. He wasn't kidding. The first week alone weeded out a quarter of our number.

Kaur was a barracks mate in my batch, a cheerful, deceptively slight figure with light brown skin and dead straight black hair. She'd also come from a regular infantry unit. We clicked on meeting and she got stuck into the training from Day One. Seems at one time it was thought that women shouldn't or couldn't serve on the front line alongside men. A couple of things changed that view. First was the capabilities of the female soldiers coming through. The second was the changing style of warfare. For the most part we were not in the line for more than a few days. Most operations were hit and run, surgical strikes, taking out installations, prisoner rescue and the like. Exfil was not usually a problem.

In the early days of the rebellion, the higher-ups tried to deal with the Sparts by using the Navy as a big hammer. Stick a capital ship in orbit above a target, press a button and wave goodbye to a city. Under the threat of a mushroom cloud, most rebels lost the will to fight. Until, of course, they called our bluff. It soon became apparent that nuking a rebel mining colony might kill the rebels but it also destroyed the facilities and rendered the place uninhabitable and non-productive for decades. And the plants, mines and factories were what the fight was all about; off world industrial resources were the lifeblood of the Terran Alliance.

Cost was a factor too. Capital ships were incredibly expensive to build. That meant the Navy were often reluctant to put even the biggest battle cruiser out on the front line. Not that there was much danger to them, the Sparts didn't have the technology to oppose the TA at that level. Let's face it, a battlecruiser cost more to build than any small mining planet would make in ten years.

Sabotage was a concern though, one strategically placed IED could put the largest ship out of action. So we ended up in a situation of having the bigger guns but not really being able to use them, hence the expansion of the forces.

Small actions were what we were being trained for.

Stratospheric Insertion, Advanced Weaponry, Small Unit Tactics, Battlefield First Aid, Bladed and Unarmed Combat. I still remember that initial BAUC session, it was where I first met Vitali.

It was a bitterly cold winter day when we were marched in to the gym, dressed for the weather in shorts and vests. There was no heating, of course, and we all stood puffing and slapping our arms. I swear there was ice on the inside of the windows. Some old mats covered the floor and the place looked like something out of the old Victorian Era. Hardly what you'd expect from an elite unit.

After the usual twenty minute wait - I never understood why the army rushes you everywhere only to then make you stand around - the door opened and a short figure with close cropped blonde hair and piercing blue eyes strode purposefully into the centre of the gym. Dressed the same as us, with a whistle round his neck, the cold didn't seem to bother him as he stood eyeing us with contempt. He blew his whistle to get our attention, placed his fists on his hips and spoke quietly in Russian accented English.

"My name is Vitali. I am here to teach you unarmed combat. You will follow my instructions to the letter. Failure to do so will result in immediate RTU. Understand?"

"Yes, sir!" we chorused. Personally, I was quite keen

to see what this little short-arse could do. I didn't have to wait long.

"We begin with breathing," he continued. "You will jog around the gym and inhale for two steps, exhale for two steps. Go!"

Go we did, following his instructions as he increased the length of the inhale and exhale. Now up to around six was okay but past that I began to struggle. Others did too. Vitali seemed to notice so he brought us back down to two, then halted us.

"Weak!" was his verdict. "You cannot breath, so how can you fight?"

There was a mumble at the back. Vitali zeroed in on the comment.

"Step forward, that man!"

The mumbler stepped out, he was a big lad with a touch of swagger about the shoulders.

"Repeat!" barked Vitali.

"Reckon I know how to fight already, don't need fancy breathing." the big lad stated.

For a micro-second a grin flicked across Vitali's face. It as a grin I was to recognise in years to come as a sign of impending trouble for someone other than Vitali. He stood to the side and gestured the lad forward.

"Show me!"

The lad shuffled out, with a bit of encouragement

from his pals. Confident now, he raised his fists and stepped towards the short instructor. He bounced around a bit on his toes, pushing out a couple of exploratory jabs. Vitali, hands down at his sides, sighed.

"We fight or we dance?"

That did the trick, the big lad scowled and moved in for a hook aimed squarely at Vitali's jaw. Trouble was, when it arrived Vitali's jaw was no longer there. The smaller man shifted slightly and did a weird ripple movement with his shoulders. His right fist popped lightly on the big lad's solar plexus. Light it seemed but the big lad dropped to his knees, desperately struggling for breath. As his attacker gulped like a goldfish out of its bowl, Vitali casually drew a knife from somewhere and ran the blunt side matter of factly across the lad's throat.

"See? Can't breath, can't fight! Now, up again, run, two steps inhale, two steps, exhale!"

We later learnt that Vitali was teaching us an old Earth Russian method of fighting, he simply called The System. This was more akin to what I'd experienced at the hands of that Landers Corporal a few years back. I took at once to the fluidity of the movements and found Vitali's breathing exercises helped with many other things, especially when it came to firearms.

Firearms... now that was pleasant surprise. We were

all used to standard issue weapons but here we were brought up to speed on more specialised kit such as beam rifles, the latest type of frag grenade and similar. We were taken through extensive fire and movement drills, small unit work and intense scenarios, some under live fire. As well as that, we were all expected to put in time on the range. While the hi-tec weapons were sexy, I still preferred the old school stuff myself, eventually setting on the latest model of AK as my go-to long. Based on a simple design that first appeared in the 20th century, the AK-110 was reliable, rugged and easy to work with a good rate of fire. I never totally trust anything that has a computer chip in it or won't work if it's raining.

We were trained up on long range target shooting too. Anyone showing real aptitude there was earmarked for potential sniper training. Providing they passed Selection, of course.

Less welcome was the fitness, bloody fitness. The level of fitness required went way beyond being an athlete. Those people have the luxury of knowing what they are training for, they can specialise. Our kind of fitness called not only for outstanding physical endurance but also the mental and psychological strength to operate at a high level of efficiency while under extreme pressure. That was where Vitali appeared again. Along with a couple of assistants, he put us through a range of tortures that stretched every man and woman to their limits. After three weeks, there were less than half of us left.

Having made it through that, we finally got to jump. Despite the technology, we were first treated to some old school training, jumping from towers to start. After that, we were told we would be taken up in a hover and were to jump out at 100 metres. Of course Kaur, being the joker asked if we could jump out lower, at which point the Jump Instructor explained that any lower wouldn't give our parachutes time to open.

"Oh," replied Kaur, "so we get parachutes, then?"

After a few jumps we were moved up to suits and finally underwent Strato Jump. Those of us who completed three SJ's were put through to Final Selection. That was a four week lovefest of marches, orientation, fire and combat drills and escape and evasion, culminating in a twelve minute continuous fight with current members of the unit. It was explained to us that the existing unit members had a vested interested in ensuring that only the best made it through, hence the last test. To be fair, they had to know the soldier beside them was up to the job, their lives may depend on it. And Landers tend not to take anyone else's word for anything, they like to be sure of it themselves.

So, in the end it was Kaur, myself and nine others

who got the coveted red beret that day, presented to us straight after by the CO, with plenty of back slapping from our new colleagues. Following that, we got a couple of days rest while our postings were sorted, followed by a week of leave.

I took the opportunity to go back home and visit Ma. It's funny how you remember a place as being okay but when you go back, it looks far more dreary and drab than you pictured. Ma was thrilled at my new job and told me how proud my grandparents would've been. They'd shipped out to this planet when they were just kids, brought by their own parents. Following the war, conditions on Earth were bad, very bad according to the history we were taught at school. Us Offworlders were all taught Earth history, let's face we didn't have much of our own.

We were taught how in the 21st century nuclear war broke out. China and America largely destroyed each other and rendered parts of the planet uninhabitable. The effect on the world economy was catastrophic, some called it a new Dark Ages. There was a long period of global unrest and conflict before governments regained control. Well, I say governments, in effect it was the large corporations who really took over.

A lot of technology was lost but necessity is the mother of invention, as a wise man once said. It was largely Europe and India that pushed us up into space. Orbiting platforms and lunar bases to start with, then moving on to Mars. The breakthrough in ship propulsion and SysGate technology allowed mankind to travel far and wide.

The corporations found no shortage of volunteers to escape the horrors of Earth. Colonies were founded, frontier settlements that then became connected by a chain of SysGates, Space Way Stations and more established outposts.   Mining operations, engineering and manufacturing plants, construction and leisure industries, all began develop throughout the Outer Colonies. Demand created supply which, in turn, created more demand. It was all run by the corporations and, of course, they extracted their pound of flesh. There was an attempt back on Earth to regain political control with the formation of the Terran Alliance. They run things on the surface now but everyone knows who the real bosses are. The suits control almost every aspect of workers' lives.

Speaking of which, given my move up the pay scale, I could now afford to help Ma move into a better place. Like most at the bottom, we lived in a corporate cube, courtesy of the local factory, with the rent being taken out of wages at source. At least she was able to have a couple of years at a nice flat overlooking the lake before she passed away.

While back home I looked up a few old pals, too, and we went out for a drink. It was clear, though, after about ten minutes that we had very little in common any more. Travel broadens the mind, I guess. So it was with no looking back that I headed to the shuttle base, transport documents at the ready.

I'd been assigned to an operational unit, Landers 3 out on the Rim. Some say it's called the Rim because it is on the edge of explored space, others because it is the arsehole of the galaxy. Personally, based on my earlier tour, I could sympathise with both points of view.

The Rim had been settled much later than the Colony Planets, most of which had two or three generations of settlers. After the asteroid dispute, dissent began to grow over working conditions. This new generation weren't so grateful, nor so submissive to their company overlords. The companies, in turn, pushed back hard. Not a good move but after so many years of a docile population I guess they had forgotten the art of negotiation. Long story short, the TA cracked down by cracking heads and that's how the conflict escalated.

That's not how we saw things at the time. Our media painted the Sparts as troublemakers. Ingrates, greedy people trying to wrest control from a beneficent government, a threat to our way of life. Having said that, there was little popular support for any kind of war. I guess the scars of the last one, Earth-bound though it was, were still fresh even after a century or so.

I'd heard that the effects of that war were still evident on Earth, though I'd never been there. It remained the heart and head of the TA, most of the elite still lived there and all the high level government and corporate headquarters were based on the old home world.

In any event, five years on and here I am, three tours in, a decorated Squadron Sergeant Major, calmly having a syg while surveying the blasted landscape of another battlefield. Job done, reports made, we meet up at the Extract Point and wait for the flyboys. An hour later and we're back on board Mother, shovelling up scran in the canteen as the transport heads back to the cruiser out on the edge of the system. The Navy never gets any closer to the action than it needs too, they are very precious about their big, expensive ships. So precious, in fact, that we are pretty much confined to quarters while on them. Perhaps they think a bunch of Landers wandering around the decks might cause trouble. They are probably right. Still, once transferred over to the big ship, we are soon homeward bound.

CHAPTER 4

CARSWELL

Home for Landers 3 is a base on Moore 5, not much to look at and basic in facilities but it's all ours. Out here on the perimeter we tend to be left alone to get on with it and that's the way we prefer things. Bureaucracy and bull are for the regular army types, the crap hats, most of them seem to thrive on it. Landers work hard and party hard. Our CO, Captain Sangha, knew that and kept a light hand on the reins. It was a few days after getting back from the last op that he called me in for a meeting.

I knocked and entered the cramped office. Captain Sangha, a short man in his early thirties, impeccably turned out as always, returned my casual salute and nodded towards the worn padded chair in front of his cheap plastiwood desk. The only other things in the office were an old style metal filing cabinet, a E-terminal on the desk and a holopic on the wall of an equally smart officer, the Captain's father, General Sangha. The Captain might be a Rodney but he was Landers through and through, from a long and illustrious line.

"Well, Mike, here's a thing." He nudged a sheet of paper towards me. I picked it up and quickly scanned the text.

"A Special Unit?"

"Yes, indeed. It's a new outfit being put together and CO's are being asked to put forward potential leadership candidates. Are you interested?"

"What's it about, Skipper?"

"Details are sketchy but it looks like small teams for sensitive missions, where precision and tact may be required."

I laughed, you had to agree that tact was not a primary Lander trait, though we could be as precise as anyone else, when required.

"What do you think, Skipper?"

"Well, you get to go in on the ground level so you may get some say in how the unit is set up. The pay is good and, if it doesn't work out you can opt to return to our warm and welcoming bosom. It will look good on your record. Put it this way, good as you are, you won't get the chance to head your own squad here for a couple of years at least."

I thought about it for a minute or so.

"Okay, Skipper, if you are for it I'll give it a crack."

" Good man, I'll let the Brass know you are up for it."

He stood and so did I, leaning forward to shake his

hand.

"Good luck, Mike. I know you'll represent us well. Don't take any bullshit from the crap hats, alright?"

"Thank you, sir!" I snapped off a sharp salute and did my best left turn and marched out of the office. Well, it does no harm to show a bit of respect now and then, where it's warranted.

So the wheels were set in motion and two days later I got a beep on my E-Pad. I was mildly surprised to find that I'd been accepted for a potential Squad Leader position, pending the selection process. The Captain had pushed my leadership qualities and battlefield experience, it seems. In any case, I had a couple of hours to pack my gear, then jumped on a transport that took me to a nearby SWS where, after a few hours wait, I was placed aboard a Navy frigate bound for Earth.

The Duty Officer informed me I was being shipped to Central Intelligence HQ on Earth, so I knew this was a big deal. I'd never actually seen the old home planet, like so many of us offworlders. I wasn't sure what to expect. I'd heard conflicting views about the place, from forested paradise to sun scorched hell hole. Not that I got to see much, being shut in cramped quarters on the ship, then called up and placed like a piece of luggage aboard a transport.

I overheard the pilot mention we were landing in

Canada. That was in North America if I remembered my school lessons correctly. Looking out as we swept in for landing, it looked like Canada had escaped the worst ravages of the war and appeared to still be covered in large swathes of forest.

If I got the job it was a going to be a new experience, being on the other side of the selection process. Though I wondered if it would be quite the same, given that the candidates selected were already highly skilled and experienced. I figured my main concern would be putting together a balanced team and to do that I needed to know the precise role of the new unit. I got my first inkling of that from Carswell,the Head Spook in charge of the whole show.

CIHQ was a place few people talked about and even fewer visited. Immediately on landing, I was ushered off the flight and into a reception area. There I was given a complete bio-metrics scan and my paperwork was gone over with a fine toothed comb. Satisfied, the grey man in the grey suit took me down a corridor to a sparse but smart office and left me there to wait. Not so much as an offer of coffee.

I was beginning to wonder if I was wasting my time when the door swished open and in strode a man in his late 50s, short reddish-blond hair thinning on top, craggy features set into a permanent scowl. And I mean permanent. I don't think I ever saw Carswell so much as crack the hint of a smile. He strode over, I stood and he grasped my hand in firm grip.

"Carswell. Sorry for the wait, as usual everything's up in the air."

I tried to place the accent, but without success, it had a kind of burr to it. Being away from Earth meant you lost your ear for that sort of thing.

"Did they offer you a coffee?" I shook my head.

"No? For God's sake." He strode over to the desk and banged a button on the intercom.

"Tom, get us two coffees in here, would you, and none of that synthi rubbish."

He sat in the plush chair behind the desk and flicked on the E-terminal, angling one screen towards himself and one towards me.

"Alright, I don't know how much you know, so I'll assume you know nothing. Now, the current military and political situation is rapidly changing. Revolt has spread all along the Rim. Independent collectives are being set up, people are resisting central control, outside interests are getting involved and stoking the situation up for their own agendas. In some cases we can solve this with negotiation. In others the appearance of a battlecruiser does the trick. However, in certain other cases we need direct, on the ground action. You have already been involved in some of that, I gather?"

He knew that full well, of course. In fact he probably knew my service history better than I did. I nodded in any case, just as the door opened and Tom came in with the coffee. Once he had gone, Carswell continued.

"So we have the Landers, of course, and units such as the Navy Strike Teams or The Pathfinders for spec ops. But this new unit is designed for very specific roles. I can't say too much more for the moment but that is the basis for the new outfit".

I took a sip of the coffee. It almost took my head off, it certainly wasn't the cheap stuff. Having been raised on synthicaf, suddenly getting the real thing was somewhat of a shock. Bearing in mind Captain Sangha's advice I said.

"With respect sir, without knowing exactly the operational parameters of the unit it will be difficult to assign personnel and roles."

"I appreciate that, Naylor. I can only advise you to follow your gut instinct. Go for good team workers with a spread of specialised skills, the best in their respective fields. This will be close in and personal work, mostly face to face and, on the whole, deniable."

I took this in and thought for a second.

"Alright, let's be clear, sir. Are we talking about

assassinations?"

Carswell choked a little on his coffee.

"The term we prefer is Termination With Extreme Prejudice. And yes, Naylor, those cards may well be on the table, so you understand the need for only the best. Is there anyone that immediately comes to mind?"

A picture of Vitali's face popped up in my mind. After Selection, I had seen him here and there and spent more than one evening over a vodka or three whenever our paths crossed. I'd also worked closely with him when I was sent back to LBA on training duties. I smiled and nodded to Carswell. "Yes, I believe I do."

The next two weeks were spent going through personnel files, speaking to the COs of various units and negotiating the Byzantine labyrinth of CIHQ. I quickly learnt that nothing bore any relation to what it was called. Take the new unit, for example. For purposes of secrecy and stealth it was to be designated *Assault Team 5*, for all intents and purposes an urban assault group whose combat role was to go in at the spearhead of an attack. That certainly could have been one of our roles but only, I found out, if there was a particular target that needed capture or neutralisation prior to the main assault going in.

In order to draw on as wide a group as possible, I'd kept parameters as broad as feasible for the recruits. Of course, they had to have sound and proven operational experience. Aside from that, I didn't care who they were, where they came from, their family background or any of that bollocks.

The one stipulation I did make was that it would be best to select from people with little or no family ties. If AT5 was going to function, we needed people on hand, ready to go at a moment's notice. The normal leave pattern for services personnel would not apply to us. I let Carswell and his team sort through all the security clearances and background bumph. My interest was purely focused on what happened at the sharp end.

In any case, I have to report that the natives were friendly, the coffee remained good and the overall view and surroundings were far more pleasing to the eye than I'd been used to for the last few years. But all good things come to an end and, so it was, that having compiled and handed over to Carswell the final list of potential candidates, he arranged for their transfer to a training facility on a planet in the Cassini System, a quiet little backwater. The pair of us set off there, along with a small admin and support team. We were scheduled to arrive two days before the recruits in order to make final arrangements.

This part of space was new to me, being closer in to the Sol System than the Landers bases. Cassini 2 was a pleasant and temperate enough planet. What threw me though, was that our new home was obviously not a military facility. On landing we were greeted by a woman who introduced herself as *Sandra*, smartly dressed, brisk and somewhat frosty. Carswell explained to me that the facility was actually owned by the Noonan Corporation and was part of their large R&D set up on the planet. I must have looked confused as he went on to tell me that Noonan were the major researcher, manufacturer and supplier to the TA and it was nice of them to let us use their place. Everyone knows you can't hide anything for long in the services so I guess it made sense, though it did raise an itch at the back of my mind.

The facilities were modern, clean and luxurious by Lander standards; there was even hot water in the showers. Hell, there were even showers! I installed myself in my own private quarters, complete with an office, and Carswell and I got to work straight away.

The pair of us, along with the admin and support team, settled in and began implementing our interview and selection process. We had decided on forty eight candidates, to be whittled down to a final twenty five to thirty. We were looking for people with specialist knowledge but who could also be flexible and operate as part of a self-contained team. Priority would be given to those who could demonstrate the ability to learn quickly, to share their knowledge and, of course, to be operationally sound.

The core of the unit would be small combat groups backed up by a Med Team, a pilot, Intelligence and Coms operatives and a Command group comprising myself and two others. That way we could keep almost everything in-house. I would be in charge of day-to-day ops and planning, with Carswell in overall control. Basically, he had the final say. I knew nothing about Carswell's background though, from his language and knowledge it was clear that he had served in some capacity prior to becoming a spook.

On Day Three transports began arriving from various locations around the TA. First off the boat was Kaur, with her dazzling smile and petite frame bowed slightly under the weight of a huge backpack. Vitali was on the second shuttle, travelling light as usual, just a small holdall and an enigmatic smile. He crossed himself on stepping off the flight, as he always did, and shook my hand warmly. By late afternoon, all the recruits had arrived and had been homed in the facility, four to a room. We let them settle in and get a bite of scoff at the canteen. Once they had finished eating, Carswell took position at the front of the room for his big welcome speech.

"Thank you for coming, ladies and gents, please sit

easy. My name is Carswell and I'm heading up this new project. Naylor here will be your Squad Commander, my eyes and ears on the ground so to speak. You have all been given some details regarding the role of this new unit, designated Assault Team 5. More will be revealed over the course of the next four weeks."

The group was silent and attentive.

"You have all been chosen because of your previous achievements, skills and knowledge. You are not here to be assessed on those skills and attributes, we know you are all capable people. What you are being assessed on, however, is your suitability for the various roles required in this outfit. You will also be taught new skills applicable to the role of this unit."

Carswell glanced around the room, making eye contact with each and every person there, including me.

"At the slightest sign that you are not suitable for this team, you will immediately be RTU'd. If you have any doubts whatsoever about working for this team, you will be RTU'd. This is not a counselling service, this is not a training course where you get a certificate at the end. You will not be shouted at, drilled, have kit inspections or be hazed. You are either in or not. If you are not, that is no reflection on your abilities, simply that you are not right for us."

He glanced over at me. "Naylor?"

I rose from my table and joined him at the front of the room.

"I'm Mike Naylor, Landers 3. As you just heard, I'm acting CO for the training and for the unit. Any issues, come to me. I know some of you hold higher rank than me but I want to make it clear that within Assault Team 5 rank is irrelevant, you are all Troopers. You will address each other by surnames. You can call me Skip or Skipper and Carswell is Chief. There will be no saluting, we will all be dressed in standard fatigues with no rank markings. For ops, a Squad Leader will be designated for each sub-team. Overall, final on the ground decisions are mine. Clear?"

The assembled nodded, like a group of kids on their first day at school.

"Okay. Any questions?"

Without giving any time for hands to be raised, Carswell immediately interjected.

"Good. For the rest of the day and evening I suggest you relax and get to know each other. Training starts 0500 tomorrow."

With that he swept out of the door as the low murmur of conversation began around the room.

CHAPTER 5

NEW FACES

I knew some of the group already, Kaur and Vitali, of course. There was also Haugen, a huge blonde bear of a man I'd worked with on a couple of previous Lander ops. Other Landers present were the lean, wiry Devlin, a Master Sniper; the always smiling Chen, an old sparring partner from my martial arts classes. There was also someone I'd not seen since BT on Krasinsky 3, the impossibly untidy figure of Douglas, now an explosives and demolition expert.

From ComMed came Dr Buresi and her assistant, Anton Woloszyk, who had served together for many months on the Rim. The Navy was represented by two Intelligence Officers, Captains Slade and Saltzmann, three coms specialists, Abomo, Javez and Miller and a group of pilots who looked to be swapping flight stories judging by the hand gestures.

Rounding out the group were personnel from the Marines, the Pathfinders, and a pair of Army survival experts. There were three CIHQ personnel, two bods from the Close Protection Squad, some police personnel, an army CQB instructor, an urban assault instructor and an older dude known simply known as *Pops*.

Some of the group chatted to people they knew or to people from the same branch. Others just sat and looked around. I made a point, with Kaur at my side, of going round and chatting individually to every man and woman there. I'm no party animal, to be honest I'm quite anti-social generally but Kaur has a winning smile and a way of getting people to open up within a few minutes. I'd already thought about having her as my 2IC, this only confirmed it.

At 0500 the next morning we were all gathered in the facility gym. There had been no reveille, no roll call, if people couldn't organise themselves, there was no place for them here. I had Vitali take the group through a 45 minute PT session then it was over to the canteen for a hearty breakfast. Following that, we had the first of our sessions from outside specialists. In this case a slight figured civilian known only to us as Mason. He began teaching us all aspects of lock picking and covert entry, from the latest systems down to old-style deadlocks.

Members of the Admin Team were constantly present, always scrutinising and making notes on their E-pads. After the evening meal I would meet with them to discuss the day's events and any issues raised. All was going well until a couple of days in, when the first cracks began to show.

It was during Vitali's session. I had asked him to take everyone through BAUC, just to sharpen up their skills and also to layer in some new attributes. He had just shown a simple evasive move followed up by a body wave that could be used to break an attacker's arm.

"No way!" came a voice from the back. Predictably, perhaps, it was one of the Marines. They are usually big lumps who have plenty of forward drive but they can suffer from what I call "tough guy syndrome". Vitali on the other hand, is small and quiet but totally nails. He called the Marine out, the man towered over Vitali.

"Grab," Vitali said and the guy did, hard and fast. Next second, there was a tearing sound and the big man cried out in agony and fell to his knees, his elbow at an odd angle. Two of the other Marines came out to help their buddy up. Vitali reached out and took the guy's E-pad as he was propped up. He logged in and made an entry, then returned the pad to the marine's belt.

"What did you write?" asked the Marine, ashen faced.

"RTU." replied Vitali impassively.

The Marine looked shocked and upset. "But why? Because I dared question you?"

Vitali looked him up and down, then around at the group before replying.

"Two reasons. First, you put yourself unnecessarily in a position where you had a good chance of getting injured. Your ego did this to you. Second, I will not serve with a man who lacks faith in me. Goodbye."

He nodded to the supporters who carried their pal off to the Med Bay. From there, he would have his gear packed and immediately be removed from the base. Vitali turned back to the group.

"Now, let us continue."

We lost more the next day. One was during the session on movement. I'd called in Lucio, a master of an old Brazilian martial art called Capoeira. I'd seen some of his work while on a cross-services exercise a year or so back and his approach impressed me. My feelings weren't shared by one of the pilots, who questioned the need for practising free and expressive movement. Lucio, who had the lithe figure and wild hair of a dancer, held the pilot in a steely gaze before replying.

"Have you ever been inside a burning ship?"

The pilot shook his head. Lucio continued, animatedly.

"Consider, then, how you might escape, in heavy heat

and flames, a small, smoke filled compartment. Consider how your terror might impact upon your movement. How your fear could act as an anchor. Consider what it is to move without fear in a bad situation, in such a way that your body is a smooth, efficient machine; unencumbered by emotion, driven only by function. This is what I teach you!"

With a toss of his hair, he turned his back on the pilot. One of the Admin Team made a note and by that evening the sky jockey was gone.

So the first week came to an end and we were already four down. The next week was centred around PsychEval, with an expert team coming in to conduct interviews and put us through various tests. We all underwent them and, I have to admit, I found the process just as intense, if not more so, than Selection. Not as physically challenging, to be sure, but in places we were all pushed to our emotional limits; in some cases beyond. The result was four more candidates RTU'd.

Following that week, we were given a day off, though I twigged very quickly there was actually no such thing as time off here. The Admin team still lurked, ever watchful. It was interesting to see how quickly some dropped their guard, particularly once the alcohol was broken out. Vitali was the most cheerful I've ever seen as the containers of booze arrived.

"About time we had some drink!" he smiled, lifting a bottle of vodka out of the silver box. "After a few drinks, people show who they really are!"

Well, that was certainly true and I guess we all needed to blow off some steam. A few drinks in and the singing began. Woloszyk produced a guitar from somewhere and it looked like the team were beginning to bond. The Admin team, of course, didn't partake but continued to observe.

A few others sat out on the edge of the group; Haugen, Devlin and the Intel guy called Kuruk. The first two I knew of old were just not the sociable type. Kuruk was new to me and, to be honest, knowing he was a CIHQ spook did not endear him to me. Still, we were there to do a job, not win popularity contests and so I didn't press the issue.

To round off the jollities, one of the Admin team rolled in a trolley covered in a range of exotic dishes. This was a big change to the standard rations we'd been served in the canteen, which was good fare but bland. Everyone tucked in, followed by more drinking and more singing. During a boisterous rendition of a filthy Navy song, I sidelined Kaur for a quiet chat.

"What's a nice girl like you doing at a party like this?" I murmured in her ear. She grinned and turned.

"What makes you think I'm nice, Naylor? You know

me better than that!"

I laughed, it was true. As demure and petite as she appeared, I'd seen Kaur roll up an enemy defence line with the grim determination of a lioness protecting its cubs. We moved into the next room where it was a little quieter.

"They seem to be getting along okay for the most part. Thoughts?" I asked.

"I agree, Mike, for the most part. Kuruk gives me the creeps though, he rarely speaks and I don't like the way he looks at me." She folded her arms instinctively.

"If it's a problem, we can get rid?"

"No, it's not that bad, I'm sure it's just me. I never feel comfortable around Green Slime. I always have the feeling they are not quite on my side."

"Can't argue with that. Remember that idiot on Tombaugh 6? Dyer, wasn't it? He'd have been more use as a paperweight. He cost us almost half the squad."

Kaur laughed and relaxed a little. "Yes, he was rather special, wasn't he? How someone can get coordinates so confused is beyond me. Dropping into the middle of the enemy compound was an interesting experience though, it saved us a tab."

"To be fair, the direct approach pays sometimes! So, be direct with me now. Anyone you think shouldn't be here?"

"Well, Javez came onto me earlier but I told her I'm not that kind of girl. I put it down to the drink and confinement. Other than that, they all seem professional and balanced. Of course, you never really know until you see people under real stress."

"True. But they have all seen action, none of them are REMFs."

"Yep. Given that, I think it's just a matter of how well they fit into the team from here on in."

"True but I think I've made my decision as to who is staying and who is going. So for some this will be their last night here."

Kaur arched an eyebrow.

"It has to come at some time. I guess better now than before we get really involved in the team work. Care to share?"

I flicked on my E-pad and tilted it towards her so she could see the list of names that would be remaining.

"Yep, I agree," she nodded. "So what next?"

"I'll inform each of the leavers quietly first thing in the morning. It's the right time to do it, Carswell is bringing in a training team from CIHQ in the next couple of days. We are going to be put through scenario training."

Kaur rolled her eyes. "Role play? God help us."

"Now, now," I chuckled. "Just think of the common good and try not to kill anyone! We'd best get back, sounds like the party is in full swing."

We returned to the main room, where even Haugen was getting into the spirit of things, roaring out some old Scandinavian drinking song to the accompaniment of much banging on the tables.

The next morning was a later start than usual, in deference to hangovers. After a muted breakfast I sent everyone back to their rooms, then made the rounds, talking to each of the RTU people quietly and individually. All took it well, most with obvious disappointment. In a couple of cases, I thought I detected relief which gave me the confidence that I'd made the right decisions.

Mid-morning I gathered the remaining group together to inform them of the situation. I congratulated them on making it into the final squad. There was much grinning and back slapping, even Kuruk cracked a brief smile. I then explained that I thought it would be a good idea for each member of the team to properly introduce themselves to the others. So over the next few days, each team member would give a short lecture on their particular field of expertise. This would help bring the group together and encourage cross-fertilization of skill sets.

Once operational, we planned that the team would be internally cross-training as much as possible. Not that we expected someone to learn how to fly a transport within a couple of weeks but at least they would know which button opened the airlock and which fired the boosters. I gave them an hour off, with the instruction to meet back in the main training room ready to speak.

CHAPTER 6

THE TEAM

Saltzmann was up first. A short, stocky character with a military buzz cut and an easy smile, he lectured the group on the basics of in-field intelligence gathering. His presentation was precise and concise, I found it very interesting as all my field work had been in the pure combat role, with any Intel piped in through the HUD.

Next up was Schrader, the one remaining pilot. He looked totally the part of flyboy, floppy blonde hair, boyish good looks and rarely seen without baseball cap or shades, or both. However, the looks concealed a professional interior. I'd read in his file about his actions in the Bell 7 crisis. Sparts had lain siege to the main TA base on the planet. Schrader had flown in and out several times, under heavy fire, to Evac all the base personnel. He gave a talk on basic piloting procedures, peppered with a few stories from personal experience. I noticed that he didn't mention the Bell 7 incident, or the gong he got for it, which only increased his standing in my eyes.

Chen was next and, as was his way, had the group in fits of laughter within minutes. Chen's heavy-set body was a living map of his service history, criss-crossed as he was with bumps, lumps and scars. Each one had a story attached and the ever beaming Chen cheerfully pointed to each in turn and told the group how he came by it. He rounded off his lecture by telling the group about the time he accidentally knocked me out attempting a martial arts stunt whilst drunk. Yes, I was the one silly enough to place the bottle on my head, Chen had assured me he could kick it off.

By contrast, Devlin's sniper lecture was technical and to the point. Devlin was a little older than me; a serious looking, dark haired man, he had a natural intensity about him. The lecture may have been dry but it was impeccably delivered. You could sense the interest from the group when he described setting up kill zones and developing the concentration required for high level sniping work. At the end, he opened the floor to questions and Saltzmann raised his hand.

"What's the most difficult shot you've taken?"

Devlin nodded and thought for a couple of moments. He glanced at me and asked, "Security clearance?"

"High level," I replied. Ever the professional, he wanted to check if he could tell the story he wanted to. He leant forward on the lectern.

"Actually, it was back on Earth, Central Europe. I had completed two tours as a sniper and was placed on secondment to the ICA for a particular operation."

"ICA?" queried Woloszyk.

"The International Crime Agency", responded Kuruk. "They are the main body responsible for combating organised crime on Earth. The drug cartels, the big crime lords, et cetera."

Devlin nodded and continued. "My target was Danilov, a major Cartel boss. They'd been trying to nail him for years but he had a very tight team around him. Usually, in these cases, the authorities can find a way in via a gang member, maybe through fear of prosecution, some leverage with their family or similar. But in this case, they had nothing. Only one person had ever come forward with evidence and he disappeared. It was later found out that Danilov had him fed to alligators. He kept a pool of them at his main compound. It was that compound I was sent to, with orders to take him out. Everything else had failed so the hit was sanctioned; in the interests of international security, I was told."

"International security?" Kaur asked. "How does that work? Wasn't he just a drug dealer?"

"A drug dealer, yes," Devlin replied, "but a very rich one, and one with increasing influence in political circles. Money buys politicians as much as it buys anything else. We also discovered that Danilov was funding Spart groups on the quiet, that put him firmly in the cross hairs as far as the brass were concerned. My cross hairs, to be precise. So I found a suitable hide up in the hills overlooking the compound and waited. There was no way I could get him while he was inside, the place had high walls and reflective glass on every window. He was a very careful man. My only chance was to get him on the way in or out."

Devlin paused to take out an light a syg. "The ICA had had eyes on the compound for weeks beforehand, so I had Intel on Danilov's routine. Two or three times a week he was driven out of the compound and away to meet various cronies, so my first thought was to hit him at one of the meeting points. But it became clear that would be too difficult. Venues were changed at the last minute and they were often in busy places with plenty of bodies around. Others were held inside offices or private houses where it would be difficult to set up an OP. So I decided to set up at the compound itself."

"Were you not worried about being seen or caught?"

asked Dr Buresi.

A rare smile flashed briefly across Devlin's features.

"No, ma'am. Camouflage and Concealment is part of our training, the most important after marksmanship. My hide was invisible beyond two metres. We had ECM in place to counter any surveillance equipment and I had a wingman set back from my position as back up and an extra pair of eyes. Then I settled in and waited. Four days, and Danilov came and went three times. Problem was, his vehicle also had reflective windows. I presumed he was in the back seat but without actual eyes on I couldn't take the shot. It was two days later that I got the break."

"He came out into the open?" asked Javez.

That ghost of a smile again. "Not exactly. Day six, the car left the compound again. I was lined up as usual, tracking the vehicle through the sights. I was fixed on the rear window but as usual it was closed. Then it happened. Danilov cracked the window to throw something out. It looked like a syg packet. A brief flash, the window was down a bit, I saw his face, I fired. Job done. The car skidded to a halt and my oppo and I packed up and left immediately. We later heard that the round had entered his right eye and blown the back of his head out."

Schrader whistled in appreciation. "Wow! That was

some shot!"

I grinned at Devlin and replied "Par for the course for a Lander, eh, Devlin?"

Devlin shrugged, "That's the job." He left the podium and returned to his seat.

It was at that moment that Carswell entered the room, followed by a slim,suited figure.

"Ah, you are all here, good. This is Mr Larsen of the Noonan Corporation. It is he who allowed us use of this facility."

Larsen stepped forward. A middle aged, grey individual in an expensive dark suit, he looked every inch the corporate man.

"You are most welcome, one and all! We at Noonan are always more than happy to help our brave service boys and girls in any way we can. I trust the facilities meet with your approval?"

Most of the group nodded dumbly, though I noticed Haugen scowled and crossed his arms.

"Splendid, splendid! Well, I won't interrupt you any further. I'm sure you have plenty of work to be getting on with. Welcome, again, and if there is anything you need, please let me know via your chap Naylor here."

He smiled like a shark and turned to Carswell.

"Excellent! Now then Gordon, what's say we have some lunch?"

It was the first and last time I ever heard anyone call Carswell by his first name. It was also the only time I saw Carswell look flustered, uncomfortable even.

"Yes, of course,Mr Larsen." He coughed and recovered his poise, turning to me and sharply commanding. "Carry on, Naylor."

With that, the pair left. Conversation broke out at once in the room, it seems I was not the only one to notice Carswell's reaction. I regained their attention by rapping sharply on the lectern.

"Alright, settle down. Two more talks then we'll break for lunch. Dr Buresi, if you please?"

The medic nodded and took the stand. Doc was a petite figure, straight brown hair, almost delicate looking, but I know she'd put in three tours with a Landers FST and had been involved in some very hairy situations.

Loading up the projector, she began running through a series of gory pictures to illustrate her talk on battlefield medicine. On the spot treatment could mean the difference between life and death and Doc described how a procedure called delayed primary suturing was used to treat bullet wounds. Most think only of covering up and putting pressure on a wound, Doc showed how you had to cut away the flesh around the path of the bullet as it carried infection which, if left covered up, could lead to serious problems later on.

I'm pleased to report that only one person needed the bin to heave in, that was our remaining cop, Tahir. Fair play, she wasn't used to the battlefield like the rest of us.

Last session of the morning went to the other member of our med team, Woloszyk. His speciality was the brain rather than the body and I was interested to see how the team would take to him. Most of us are generally wary of trick cyclists and shrinks, or Wizards as they are known. It was obvious though that our guy, quickly christened Wiz, knew his stuff.

He looked the bookish type, round shouldered, hands usually in pockets, but he talked with real passion about his work with PTSD sufferers and the need to address issues head on before they became major problems. He tied in his talk with many of the things Vitali had taught us about dealing with fear. I know the image is of tough, fearless warriors but there's no place in my unit for anyone who says they are never afraid. Those types are usually the first to crack.

Wiz made it clear that his door was always open and that he would be running constant psychevals on the unit. He was also trained as a crisis negotiator, which gave another string to the team's bow.

Post lunch, we had four more talks starting with

Abomo. One of the few Earthers amongst us, he was a tall, willowy African man with an engaging sing-song accent. He began on the basics of battlefield communication before developing into his real passion, electronic surveillance and counter-surveillance. His talk was precise, concise and practical.

After that, Javez, curvy, long haired and grinning, took up the coms thread and ran with it. Her speciality was encryption and codes, formulating and breaking. Her presentation style was much more laid back than Abomo but no less practical.

Following her was Jacobs, an Army survival instructor. Weather-beaten, lean, dark hair pulled back tight, she certainly looked the part, lecturing us on cold weather survival. I later wondered if she had some prior knowledge of a forthcoming mission or if it was just one of those odd coincidences.

Haugen took the next slot and, I'll admit, I wondered what the grizzled, blonde bear of a man would talk about. He surprised me by talking about the value of camaraderie and team work in a unit.   Like a couple of the previous speakers, he peppered his talk with various examples from his service history, finishing with a moving account of having to leave a wounded comrade in a precarious situation. I swear there were more than a few in the group dabbing their eyes at that. Not me, I just had some dust in my eye.

Another meal break and we scheduled four more talks to round the day off. My old pal Douglas began the evening sessions with a lecture on explosives, how and when to use them. Douglas was the sort of man who could make the smartest suit or uniform look like a sack of shit tied in the middle. He had reduced Sergeant Majors to tears, so slovenly was his appearance. His hair stuck up at odd angles,his fingernails were always dirty and he had a nice collection of canteen medals on his shirt. Added to that, he was suffering a severe case of nerves. He was sweating before he started and stammered his way through the introduction. I had to laugh, the thought of public speaking obviously terrified the poor man. Yet I've seen him snip the wire on an IED without a second's hesitation or so much as a tremor in the hand.

I think his nervousness endeared him to the group and, once he got into his stride, he was fine.

Pops was up next. I'd never met him before this gathering but he was something of a legend amongst the community. He had started in the regulars before going into Landers and ending up in various Spec Ops outfits. What he didn't know wasn't worth knowing and I'd brought him into the group precisely for that reason. He was by far the oldest person there. Most of us were around the thirty mark, he must have been nudging fifty, though he looked older. A tough life will do that to you.

He took the lectern looking like an old fashioned Earth pirate with his curly, collar-length hair, salt and pepper beard and non regulation earring. He grinned at the group, winked at Kaur and began. He ran with Douglas' explosives theme, though from an IED and booby trap perspective rather than demolition. In short order he ran through what to look for and where and how to set the main types of IED. He finished his talk with a little reaction test, cleared with me beforehand, rolling a dummy grenade down the aisle between the chairs. Once everyone was back in the room they did see the funny side. It was hard not to with Pops.

Dutton followed. I'd crossed paths briefly with him once before, his primary work these days was on Close Protection. Unlike the stereotype of the huge bodyguard, Dutton was the quintessential grey man. Average height, average looks, quietly spoken, nothing about him seemed remarkable. But once he began to talk us through the basics of CP and had us doing some exercises on observation and awareness, his skill shone through.

Last speaker for the day was the remaining NI Officer, Slade. If Dutton was the grey man, Slade was at the opposite end of the spectrum. Flame red hair, over two metres tall and looking, to my mind, like some kind of grinning stick insect. His colleague had already covered the basics of their trade, so Slade decided to go completely off-piste.   He told us of his passion for old films, particularly 20th century movies. He gave a brief history of cinema then announced he had a special treat for us, the showing of a classic film from that time. I'd arranged for the film to be loaded into the room's display system and, at a nod, one of the Admin team dimmed the lights and a screen slowly whirred down behind the podium. Slade returned to his seat and for the next two hours we all relaxed and watched the movie. Admin even brought in some drinks and snacks.

I have to say it wasn't my cup of tea. I got confused. The Sparts were the good guys. The bad guys were dressed in white, except for their leader, who was dressed in black. They were terrible shots, too; while the heroes, who seemed to lack any military training, scored a hit every time.

The funniest thing for me was seeing those old 20th century ideas of what spaceships would look like. They were either lumbering, skyscraper like dreadnoughts bristling with turrets, antennae and dishes, or sleek fighters screaming through space spitting laser beams. If only the makers could have seen our ships, dull grey slabs for the most part, looking more like a garbage scow than a gun-covered warship. Still, the group all cheered at the end even though the Sparts won; a fact which didn't go down too well with Admin, judging from the looks on their faces. The cheering even woke up Dutton who, as we soon found out, took every opportunity to take a nap.

We filed into the canteen for dinner, most of the group chatting animatedly about the movie. It was good to see most members of the team beginning to mix, with the usual exceptions. I was barely halfway through my bland, but no doubt nutritionally balanced, dinner when Carswell beeped me to go see him in his office.

Three people, a man and two women, were already there waiting for me. Carswell introduced them as John, Joe and Betty from CIHQ Training Division and explained they were the team who would be running the forthcoming scenario exercises. They wanted to run through each team member with me and highlight any potential flash points, weaknesses to be probed or strengths to be developed. By the time I finished there it was close to midnight. The three spooks left for their quarters and I was thinking about turning in myself, given that I had to be up again in around five hours. Before I left the room I turned to Carswell.

"You make a lovely couple."

"What? Who?"

"You and the Noonan guy. What was his name again?"

"Larsen. Mr Larsen. Do you have a point, Naylor?"

"Just that it seems odd having a company man dropping in on a top secret military operation."

"I thought I explained all this. We are occupying a Noonan facility, they are helping us out. Listen, Mike, you take care of the team. Let me deal with the suits. Okay?"

Carswell had never addressed me by my first name before, I wasn't sure whether to be pleased or worried. In any event, I had made my feelings clear, so I nodded and returned to my room.

CHAPTER 7

SMALL VICTORIES

At 0500 hours next morning, the group gathered for PT, followed by breakfast, then combatives with Vitali. The rest of the day was taken up by the remaining lectures. First up were the two Marines, Armstrong and McNulty. Although typical looking, slab-like Marines, the pair had shown keen tactical thinking during the course and had worked extensively together on various spec ops, which I figured was an advantage.

Some said they were paired up in more ways than one. Well, that was none of my business. People pairing up is not unusual in the Services, after all we are pretty much a self contained world, so it's only natural that relationships are formed. Sometimes they are brief flings, sometimes I guess it's a form of stress relief. Funny enough, though we'd worked together for a long time, there was never any hint of anything like that between Kaur and myself. I guess chemistry is there or not, and she always felt more like a sister to me.

Having couples serving together was a little more unusual and I wasn't sure how I felt about it. On the one hand, they certainly knew how to live with each other, something you have to take into consideration when you are on ops and working in very close proximity for days or weeks. On the other hand, would they argue, what if personal feelings got in the way of duty? In the end I figured best thing was to see how things went. I didn't want to split the pair up as they came highly recommended.

After watching their presentation, I could see why. Using kit they had brought with them, they gave us a display of weapons handling and deployment, ranging from old style bolt action weapons up to some of the latest equipment. As Marines are wont to do, they made a lot of noise and there was little subtlety. But they obviously knew their stuff and I viewed them as assets for the team. Sometimes you need a little muscle.

The morning was rounded off with fieldwork. The group was driven out to the nearby countryside, where our pair of Army survival experts gave demonstrations of camouflage and stealth. Williams was tall and rangy, with thinning sandy hair and piercing green eyes. A man of few words, I think he preferred the company of trees and nature to humans.

Khan was about the same height as Williams but carried a little extra weight and had a ready smile and an easy going way about him. The pair had worked together previously and ran us through the ins and outs of field obs, along with some simple wood craft exercises.

Our third expert, Bahadur, was from Pathfinders, a specialist recce unit. He had prepared an outdoor tracking and weather obs exercise for the group. Once ready, he called us over and ran us through the rules of the drill. Stood atop a fallen tree trunk, the swarthy figure looked very much at home in this environment, large hunting knife in his belt, colourful bandanna atop his head (which some team members claimed was to hide a growing bald spot). In any case, he conducted a thorough briefing and the rest of the day was taken up in his Hare and Hounds exercise.

Everyone got caught in the end, apart from Dutton. He turned up later at the RV, a sheepish grin on his face.

"You were well hidden!" Williams told him. "We covered the search area thoroughly, how'd you manage it?"

Dutton rubbed his chin. "Yeah, well, I got myself dug in at a nice little spot, covered myself over with foliage and er… well, I nodded off. Only just woke up fifteen minutes ago."

The team laughed, Williams just shook his head. Bahadur clapped Dutton on the shoulder.

"Good work. You see, remember I told you about concealing intention as well as your bodies? Now, I'm not saying you should fall asleep to hide but there is a point to take note of here."

That evening we were back at base and the topic went from lo to hi-tec, with Mir from CIHQ up first. A quietly spoken, studious type, with silver grey hair despite his young age, he took us through the latest developments in personal electronics from a coms and surveillance perspective, as well as giving us a brief outline of data hacking.

Tahir was next, a sharp eyed woman in her mid-30s with, what I later found out, was called a bindi on her forehead. Tahir was unique in that she was the only non-forces personnel here. Her background was police work, in some of the toughest areas back on Earth. I liked her humour, she stood at the lectern with a coffee and a doughnut as if to live up to the cop stereotype.

She described her work, with an emphasis on surveillance of the old fashioned kind, staking out suspects and the like. It was an interesting perspective for the rest of us. Tahir was used to working within a totally different set of parameters and I could see how she could be invaluable in certain situations, especially when dealing with civvies.

The day's sessions were rounded off by Kuruk. He stood motionless behind the lectern for a couple of minutes, gazing out over the group like some kind of gaunt, cadaverous schoolteacher. Then he began and, to my surprise, I found myself enthralled. He expanded on Saltzmann's earlier theme of Intel gathering, taking it away from purely battlefield operations and into the wider scheme of pre-Ops planning and long term strategy formulation. By the end of it, I had a new understanding and deeper respect for the man and his work. Not too much though, he was green slime still, after all.

That just left one more day of lectures. Vitali was already known to the group through his training sessions, and I knew he disliked public speaking, so I let him off the hook. So I prompted Weaver to take the first session, at the indoor firing range that had been set up for us.

A powerfully built, totally bald, black guy, he moved with an easy fluidity and impressed all with his pistol handling skills. I knew he was no slouch at hand-to-hand as well, having partnered up with him during some of Vitali's lessons.

The final sessions were myself, Kaur and Koenig.

Koenig was a tough,wiry looking individual. Like most of us he favoured a crew cut but he had the most body hair I've ever seen on an individual. Thick and black, along his arms and back, though he always kept his face clean shaven. He was an Urban Assault trainer and ran us through the fundamentals of room clearance and FIB.

His lecture done, I touched heads with Kaur and we decided to present a joint lecture on the history of Landers, from the first jumps in the first half of the 20th century, when Russian paras actually jumped off the wings of old prop planes, through to the major operations of World War Two and beyond. Then, on to the establishment of the modern Landers groups and an outline of more recent operations.

We took pains to stress that although the tech may have changed, the job and the people remained the same. Not a particularly practical lecture, I admit, but I felt it was good to give the unit some perspective and also a feeling of having roots. After all, the deeper the roots, the stronger the tree.

Lectures over, we gave the team the night off to relax and do whatever they liked, although they were confined to base until the end of the course. A unit needs to bond socially as well as professionally and Kaur and I were glad to see that happening. The piss-taking had already started. Seems that Mir had made the mistake of letting slip that he didn't like spiders, so certain other team members had done their best to find as many of the critters as they could. Like on so many On many colony planets, all sorts of bugs had made the trip with us humans and established their own outposts. Added to that was the local flora and fauna, of course.

In any event poor Mir now ran the gauntlet of spiders on his dinner plate, in his kit, his cot and anywhere else twisted minds could think to put them. As we came in he was jumping up and down shaking his shirt, shouting "Get it off me! Get it off me!" while Bahadur and Chen were in fits, Chen winking at me and whispering, "It's just a bit of thread."

The next day saw the start of the scenario training. John, Joe and Betty were sat at the head table, watching impassively as we all filed in an sat down. Betty began proceedings, closing the folder in front of her and declaring, in a loud voice, "One of you is a spy."

Everyone immediately looked to the left and right and began murmuring. I groaned inwardly. Days of working this group into a team and within five seconds this idiot had sewn the seeds of paranoia. As things progressed over the next few sessions, though, I began to appreciate the approach of the scenario team.

Beginning with basic personal observation and body

language skills, they began running the group through more and more intricate scenarios, ratcheting up the pressure each time. Another aspect of their training was teamwork, seeing how the group worked in pairs, threes, or larger units. Part of this included putting teams into very cramped conditions for extended periods of time, always giving them tasks to do, not letting them sleep or rest. I'd seen and experienced similar before, of course, during my own selection but these guys had it down to a fine art.

It may seem an odd thing to outsiders but any unit spending extended field time together really needs to have its shit together before going active. You have to be aware of each other's attitudes, habits, which buttons to avoid pressing. In the field you will get intimately acquainted with each others' sights, sounds and smells, so it's best to sort out any issues beforehand.

Kaur and I watched this part of the process particularly closely. Ribbing is one thing; arguments, bullying or fights are something else. If they flare up on ops you can have a real problem on your hands. Of course, we had to join in on all the training too, a team has to respect it's commanding officers; and that respect, particularly with experienced individuals, has to be earned.

This stage of the training was rounded off with three

days on interrogation methods, both developing and resisting. The training staff explained that we may well be working undercover, with no immediate back up. Of course, everyone and anyone can be broken by interrogation, their main goal was to get our people to a stage where they could resist questioning for 24 hours. Following that, if we knew a unit member had been captured and compromised, then we would change our mission plan in any case, rendering any info given largely useless.

On the flip side, knowing how to get information from a prisoner is also a vital skill. People from outside tend to think it's a case of slapping someone round a bit or threatening to cut off fingers, or worse. Well, that can work but, as we found out, it's a much deeper subject than that. Sometimes the carrot works better than the stick.

Before being sent out on a training exercise, the whole team underwent one last round of medical checks. It was during this stage that we received our sub-dermal chips, courtesy of Noonan.   A pair of medical technicians came in to administer the implants. The latest model, we were told, NFC chips with built in security protocols that would see us through most security checkpoints without the need for paperwork. None of us was too happy about it, apart from our resident tec-head Javez, but orders were orders. On the plus side, a few of us were thrilled to discover that by waving our arms around in front of it, we could now get the gedunk machine in the lobby to drop its treasure at no cost. Small victories.

CHAPTER 8

THE MAJOR

I was pleased to report to Carswell that the scenario stage of training had gone well, we'd had no more RTU's. The team was beginning to bond, roles and boundaries were being established. Carswell nodded in approval, confirmed my position as Squad Leader and gave us all a couple of days off. After that, he had organised our final training exercise - we were to mount an intel gathering raid on Hoyle 4, a Marine Corps base in one of the inner systems. Being Marines, of course, we knew this would be no walkover. They were one of the old US Marine units too, so there was a considerable amount of prestige and face involved. We had a couple of days planning, which we put to good use, then a transport arrived to take us up to the Navy frigate that was to be our ride for the mission.

On the face of it, it looked straightforward enough. Gather five pieces of Intel at specific locations, while evading capture. We all knew, though, that looking straightforward was part of the test and there would no doubt be plenty of curve balls thrown at us to test our mettle. We planned accordingly, paying particular attention to the rules of engagement and how we might bend them. As far as I was concerned, there was only ever one rule; complete the mission as efficiently as possible and with as few casualties as possible. Anything else was army bullshit.

As this was a training mission and the unit did not technically yet exist, we were confined to quarters on the frigate. Not the most luxurious of berths but we were all used to worse out in the field. So we made the most of the time to run through the plans again and again. Finally, we were deposited planet-side at a transit station some distance from the Marine base. I was due to have a meeting with the base CO and umpire team that night and then the team would move into positions the next day. Forget that, I had them move out that night, so we had eyes on the base while they were making their preparations.

Kaur and I attended the meeting, which turned out to be a dinner at the Officers Mess on the base. A staff car picked us up and dropped us at the guardhouse, where we were escorted by two very well turned out and very tall marines to the Mess. All conversation stopped as we were shown in and most of the assembled eyed our plain fatigues with some distaste. The Umpire Group were already there, enjoying the hospitality. From the looks of it, they were all old friends. A ruddy, brash figure in immaculate dress uniform strode over and introduced himself as Major JT Donaldson. He welcomed us to the base, told us he looked forward to a good exercise, then waved a hand at the assembly behind him and bade us take our places at the table. The spread was laid out in full silver service, they were obviously making a big show.

The game playing started from the off. Silly little things, you know, the chairs we were given were a little lower than everyone else's. Kaur was virtually at face level with the table. The waiter spilled soup on my sleeve as he served, the aide made a point of pointing out which cutlery we should use. So I deliberately made a point of slurping loudly as I ploughed through the soup, then belching loudly in appreciation when I was done. Kaur didn't know where to look and kicked me sharply under the table. Fuck it, if they wanted to rattle us they would have to try harder than that.

Following dinner, brandy and cigars were produced and the Major bade us follow him. He took us around the mess, pointing out holopics on the wall, telling us the stories behind them and the various bits of paraphernalia set in display cases. We finished at the unit's Roll of Honour where, with a flourish of his cigar, he laid out his stall for us.

"See," he said, draining and putting down his brandy glass, "this here's a real, top flight military unit. Now don't get me wrong, I'm sure you special forces types are good at hiding out in the woods and observing things. But our people here..."

At this point he puffed out his chest with pride. "Well, boy, our people here are real soldiers, every last one of them. Marines! Warriors, finely tuned, we run like a well oiled machine."

Kaur and I made polite noises. He continued and I glanced at my watch. He didn't know our team were already in place and waiting for my word. A discrete press on the E-pad in my pocket and the signal was given. The Major concluded his little speech with a hearty handshake to both of us. He even patronisingly wished us "Good luck". We bade our goodnights to the Umpire Team, then the two wooden tops appeared to escort us back to the car and, within minutes, we were back at the gate.

The next morning saw Kaur and I sat in place at our

makeshift CP in the woods overlooking the base. We watched as squads of marines came out to form perimeter patrols, followed by APCs rolling out of the main entrance to sweep the surrounding countryside. It was about an hour later that we were picked up. One of the sweep squads came crashing through the undergrowth and discovered our cunningly concealed tent. We were tagged and bagged, none too gently, by a grinning corporal, marched to the nearby APCs then driven down to the base.

On arrival another pair of marines - they could have been the doubles of those on duty last night - pulled us out of the APC and, again, none too gently, shoved us along a corridor and into Major Donaldson's Ops room. He was in place, holding court, two of the umpires with him. Around the room operatives sat at screens, two more marines stood guard at the door. There were no other exits or windows in the place. No way out, our fate looked sealed. Our two guards stood looming behind us as the Major came over grinning.

"Well, I did tell you, Naylor. Proper soldiers! Did your people even turn up? We haven't seen hide nor hair of them. Hell, I don't blame them, must be quite intimidating the thought of taking on the Marine Corps!"

I shrugged and said nothing. What could I say? It was then that one of the tec operatives spoke.

"Major, there's something odd happening."

The Major span round. "What do you mean, soldier?"

"Our surveillance seems to have gone down, sir. And our computer system… it appears to have been hacked sir, all our data is disappearing. I don't know where it's going!"

Kaur coughed. "Actually, it's going to our temporary server, sir. Don't worry, we will replace the data once the exercise is over."

"What, I don't understand, how…"

Kaur explained. "We placed our equipment last night and gathered most of the intel required while your troops were asleep. Our people triggered the data hack on seeing our capture."

The Major was lost for words. Before he could protest further, I delivered the punch line.

"Oh, and you are now our prisoner, sir. If you could relinquish your firearm and accompany us?"

He stiffened at that and I felt the two guards behind us make a move. That was cut short by the two guards at the door, actually Armstrong and McNulty, swiftly disarming then cuffing them.

The tec who'd raised the alarm stood and grinned, coming over to us.

"Good work Javez," I told her. "Any problems?"

"No, Skip. All alarm systems have been neutralised

and coms from this room cut."

"Okay, let's take our prize and leave, shall we?"

The rest of the tecs stood, revealing themselves as Weaver, Slade and Saltzmann. I thought the Major was going to burst a blood vessel. He turned to the umpire.

"This is not right, they cheated! The exercise was to supposed start this morning!"

The umpire, tired no doubt of being in the Major's presence for so long, merely shrugged.

"I can see no infraction of rules. Your opponents are an irregular unit, after all, you can't expect them to operate like regular troops."

Khan and Abomo entered the room, both resplendent in marine uniform.

"Just like old times, eh?" Khan laughed to our two tame marines. They preened slightly, Armstrong pointing to the Major.

"Yes, and I remember this prick from my time in the Corps. A pleasure to meet you again, sir!" he laughed in the Major's face.

McNulty said to me, "The rest of the team are waiting in an APC waiting outside, Skip. Suggest we bundle up our friend here and make our exit?"

I nodded and in no time at all we were driving off base, our galloping Major firmly trussed up in the back. His men had not been too gentle with us, so I felt no compunction to be too gentle with him.

Taking him back to our place was not strictly part of the exercise but we thought having him as a guest for a day or so might make a point. We even let him sit in on the debrief, explaining exactly how we had infiltrated his base the night before, neutralised his command room staff and, in effect, taken over his base without firing a shot. I'd even got hold of his personal brandy stock. I don't think he appreciated it.

The exercise marked the end of the selection process and I was pleased to inform everyone they had made the grade. Once back at our training base there was nothing left to do but have a drink to celebrate. And this time it was a real booze up, there were no observers taking notes. Even Carswell popped his head round the door.

"Let them have some time off," he told me. "I'll be getting details of your move to your own base shortly."

"Cheers, Boss." I lifted my glass in salute before knocking back the contents. A warm, rosy glow spread throughout my limbs. "Mmm, good brandy. We should kidnap Majors more often."

Carswell gave a scowl. "Don't! I'm still dealing with the fallout from that, it's cost me a fortune replacing his drink. Alright, we'll speak soon."

With that, he was gone and I turned back to the

celebrations, which currently centred around an Army versus Navy drinking contest.

A week later saw us en route to our new home. We were transported in to Hawking 2, a backwater planet in centrally placed system. I'd like to say the Brass had splashed out and built us a state-of- the-art base, fully geared to our requirements, but this is the army we're talking about. What we had was an old mothballed regular unit base, left empty after the cutbacks. It was drab, dusty and stank like a locker room. The clean up began straight away, starting with our quarters.

As this had been a full unit base, we had the luxury of separate rooms, along with a couple of rec areas and training rooms, a canteen and a kitchen facility. A couple of licks of paint and the place started looking brighter, though we never completely got rid of the smell.

The planet was a minor manufacturing centre, with a large town quite close to the base. Much of the workforce was migrant, moving on and off planet as labour demands rose and fell, so the appearance of "strangers in town" would not be unusual. A former military base being reactivated might draw more attention, so Carswell had set up a dummy private security company as cover. *Vigilance Security* proclaimed the shiny new sign at our front gate. It was close enough to the truth for none of us to need briefing and dull enough to discourage anything more than a casual interest.

The guards on the gate were all CI personnel and were housed in their own block on the other side of the base. As well as perimeter security, they were also to take care off all local matters in terms of supplies and utilities. Carswell offered us the use of an army catering team but I turned it down, we could do all our own cooking. The fewer outside personnel we had on base, the better, as far as I was concerned.

The base had its own landing strip and hangar set up, important as we would much rather have our own transport close to hand. I put Schrader in charge of the whole thing. He grabbed in some guys he had worked with before to form a mechanics team, who quartered in with the security bods. When I checked in with him, he was keen to show me his latest acquisition. Wiping his hands on a rag, he proudly gestured to the transport ship behind him.

"How about that, Skip, ain't she a beaut?"

I nodded vaguely, it looked like a museum piece to me. Grey, streaked, I swear there was moss growing out of one panel line. What was the old expression? *Twenty thousand rivets flying in loose formation...*

"I know she doesn't look much but this is a T-220, the best of the Tupolev series. It's got a low profile for ECM, plenty of storage, will carry twenty-five plus crew and has an EV of 18k per second, that's with a full load. I'll get the team to tune her up and we'll add a few little extras in, too, maybe some cannons for ground support."

I nodded again, none the wiser. Schrader laughed.

"Yep, I know, she looks a mess. But I figured it was better to have something that wouldn't stand out, no military markings, no pack drill."

I couldn't argue with that, so I left the flyboy to tend to his new love and made my way over to the gym. I'd arranged to liaise with Weaver and Vitali to organise a training rota to keep everyone sharp. They were also cooing over new toys, though in their case it was sidearms. Most of the requested kit had arrived that day on a pair of Navy shuttles.

I'd asked each unit member to provide a list of requirements and touched Carswell for the requisition orders to pay for them. Some of the team already had their own personal kit, some jumped at the chance to get new. Our ethos was that people should always use the gear they are most comfortable with - within mission parameters of course.

My next stop was the Coms Centre, where Saltzmann and Javez were rummaging through a stack of crates and boxes as Slade ticked off an inventory.

"Looks expensive." I nodded to him as various

consoles and gadgets were unpacked. "How did you stretch Carswell's budget to get all this lot?"

Slade grinned. "Well, Skip, let's just say I know a few people. It's amazing what falls out the back of a transport."

"Don't tell me," I raised a palm. "What I don't know can't hurt me!"

Saltzmann wandered over, laughing. "Don't tell Kuruk, either. He's already asking for invoices and receipts."

My last call was to Doc and Wiz, they were also busy unpacking crates and boxes.

"All okay, Doc, got everything you need?" I asked as I entered the Med Bay.

Buresi looked up from her unpacking. "All fine, Skip. Once everything is set up I'll organise a check up rota for the team and a diet and exercise plan. Wiz is going to arrange regular one-to-ones with everyone."

I nodded in approval and headed off to my quarters. Nothing too grand, a bunk room with en suite and an office. Still, it was more privacy than I'd been used to up to now. I'd already unpacked my few belongings, stowing them away and putting the couple of pics I had on the desk. I'd just fired up my console and started the unwelcome work of sorting through my admin when Pops knocked and stuck his head round the door.

"Alright, Pops? Fancy a drink?"

"Good lad," he grinned, parking himself in the chair opposite as I got a bottle of brandy and two glasses out of the drawer.

"Cheers!" We clinked glasses and Pops leaned back in the plastic chair.

"So, what's bugging you, Pops?" I recognised the look, seen it before in military types. We tend not to be too open about our feelings but you learn to read the signs after a while.

"I'm not sure, Skip. There's an itch at the back of my head that I can't quite scratch. Doesn't it seem odd to you that this unit is put together at this time, what with all the debate going on in the Senate?"

"I don't really follow politics much, Pops. To be honest, I find they all say the same thing and seem to be mostly out for themselves."

Pops nodded and took another slug of the warming liquor. "Well, I can't argue with that. But I've been stationed on Earth for the last couple of years. In fact, I've been at the heart of it. I was on President Theodorou's Close Protection detail for a while. She's no fan of extending the war, I can tell you. She's always pushed for negotiation with the Sparts, a diplomatic solution. Her opponents, though, are pushing for an expansion of the war effort, more ships, more troops.

Which means more contracts for the companies who supply them, of course."

"What's this got to do with us, then?"

Pops furrowed his brow. "I'm not sure, Mike. Call me cynical, but I wonder if we are going to see an increase in terrorist attacks across the systems. You know how it works?"

"Problem, reaction, solution, right?" I poured us both another snifter.

"Yep. Anyway, it's just an itch. At the end of the day we go where we're told and do what we have to, like the good soldiers we are, right?" Pops grinned and raised his glass.

"Good soldiers... I'll drink to that. And I'll bear in mind what you said. I'll not have this team taken advantage off for someone's profit or political career."

We clinked glasses and drank. Pops still seemed to have something on his mind.

"Is there anything else?" I asked him.

He paused for a second, then shook his head.

"No, Skip, that was it. I'll be off, wouldn't want to stop you doing your filing." With a smile, he was gone.

CHAPTER 9

HOSTAGE

We didn't have to wait too long for our first op, only a couple of weeks, in fact. An alert arrived from Carswell; a hostage situation on Hirayama 5, a neighbouring system. I assembled a team and told Schrader to ready our transport, christened *Lady Luck* judging by the name and pair of dice now painted on the nose cone. Hirayama was only one jump away, we'd get off planet and hitch a lift from passing Navy. I brought the group up to speed en route.

"Hostage situation. We have a disaffected individual holed up in the local government offices. Believed to be armed, he is holding six members of staff hostage."

"Local plod unable to deal with it?" asked Slade.

"Local LEO are virtually non-existent," Kuruk interjected. "Due to the almost total lack of crime on Hirayama 5 and successive budget cuts, there is little more than a token force in place at the main population centre. The planet largely houses admin staff and a Navy shipyard."

"And I'm guessing the Navy don't want to get involved?" asked Khan, raising his eyebrows at Slade.

"Probably not, but that's why I've brought you along." I responded, looking at Slade. "You're to liaise with the Navy staff, find out what's what. Kuruk, I want you to gather as much Intel as you can on this guy... name of Jareth Kadis. I've pinged the details over to you just now."

Kuruk nodded and turned to his E-pad.

I continued around the rest of the team.

"Pops, Weaver, Khan, you're with me. Javez, I want you to oversee any surveillance that's going on and grab any plans or schematics you can of the building. Wiz, you're on negotiation duties. Doc, I want you to knock up a strong sedative if you can, in case we can get close enough to this guy to administer."

At that point Schrader's voice came over the intercom. "Approaching gate now, jumping in ten minutes. Buckle up boys and girls, once we're through it will be a couple of hours to landing."

After touching down at the main city airbase, we were met by the local LEO brass and rushed through, lights and sirens blaring, to the scene. A non-descript office building sat surrounded by a collection of police vehicles, a flock of media vans and a gaggle of onlookers. Slade spotted someone he knew and moved off towards a group of three Naval officers present. I was led to the officer overseeing the operation, a tired looking blonde lady who introduced herself as Commisioner Hendriksen.

She gave me the sitrep. The guy had walked into the office 20 hours ago, just as it was closing. He rounded up the staff and, as far as we knew, was holding them all in the main office on the first floor. All points of entry had been locked, blinds were down on all the windows, there was no way of knowing exactly who was where.

"Is he acting alone? Is he armed?" I asked.

Hendriksen nodded. "We think he is on his own. There have been no indications of anyone else being involved. From the security footage we know he at least has one weapon, some kind of rifle."

"Has there been any communication? Does he have demands?"

"Limited. He asked for food and water to be put at the front door. We complied and someone, one of the staff we believe, picked it up."

"Did you think to drug the food? Lace it with sedatives?"

"We did, but I was advised against it by my superiors.

They felt it would be too risky, in case he had someone else try the food first. At this stage, my orders are to keep the man happy and to contain the situation until, well, until you arrived."

"Anything else?"

"Yes, he said he has political demands which he would let us know later."

"Later? What's he waiting for?"

Hendriksen shrugged. "Who knows?"

I nodded. "And the media? How did they get wind of it?"

Hendriksen scowled. "Not from my end. I was working to keep this low key. First I knew is when one of those vans turned up about an hour ago, followed by three more just now. I've kept them well back but they are quite insistent."

At that point, Kuruk and Javez came over. I asked Hendriksen if there was somewhere we could conflab and she gave us use of her command vehicle.

"Alright, what do you have?" I took a seat at small desk in the back of the CV.

Kuruk read from his notes. "Jareth Kadis, aged 32. Born Messier System out on the Rim. Occupation, factory worker. Has a criminal record, all low level stuff, petty theft, small time drug dealing. Fired from his job a couple of months back. Married, separated, three children. All live with the mother on Messier 7."

"Any political affiliations, history of violence? Military background?"

"None as far as I can see. Messier has some minor political agitation going on but it's hardly a Spart hotbed. As for Kadis, no military service, no convictions for violence."

"Okay, thanks. Javez?"

Javez had been busy at the printer and turned toward me with sheets of paper.

"Here's floor plans of the building, courtesy of the local authorities. Standard stuff, very little in the way of security, should be easy enough to get in and out."

"Good. Any chance of eyes on?"

"Not much. There is a camera at the main entrance, that's pretty much it. I have an idea, though?"

"Go on."

"Well, if the group is in the main office, it is likely filled with a number of computer terminals. Assuming they have been kept switched on and assuming I can hack into the mainframe, I may be able to get access to the inbuilt cameras in the monitors."

"Cameras?" I asked. Tec was never my strong point.

"Yes," Javez continued. "Standard issue in this kind of facility, so that staff can conference face to face without having to leave their desk. If I can get in, it won't give us much but we will at least get some view of what's going on."

"Okay, get to it." Javez turned and began unpacking equipment from her bag. Slade poked his head round the rear door of the CV.

"Nothing much from the Navy bods, Skip. Our man is unknown to them, records pick him up as having come into the system four days ago on a regular passenger transport. No known family or acquaintances here. He stayed at a cheap motel a few blocks away. They've searched the room, it was clean."

"Thanks, Slade, stick with the Navy, will you? Let me know if you pick up anything interesting." He nodded and disappeared. I stepped outside into the bright sunlight again and, grabbing Pops and Weaver, decided to take a tour around the perimeter. Hendrksen had done a reasonable job with what she had. The locals had formed a security cordon, any movement in our out of the building would be spotted. Most of the locals were armed but only with handguns. Two officers with shotguns covered the main entrance. A noise overhead made me look up. A hover was slowly buzzing just over the building. A cameraman was half hanging out the side door, getting a good shot of the scene below. More media, it seemed. I called Hendriksen over and pointed up.

"Can we do something about that?

She scowled. "Not much, to be honest. I can try and apply local aviation laws but we have to get them back down first. Freedom of the press and all that. Speaking of which, the media are asking for a statement. Do you want to do a press conference?"

The thought of it flipped my stomach. "No. You do it. Tell them the situation is under control, give them minimal information about the suspect and please don't mention me or any of my team."

"Got it," Hendriksen replied. "Feel free to use my CV as your own, I'll have some food and drink sent over for you."

I thanked her and went back in to see how Javez was doing. She was sat scowling in concentration, her face green in the glow of the monitor. I didn't interrupt, just left her to it. Then Kuruk called me over, showing me his E-pad.

"Local news," he said. "This is going out live."

On screen, a reporter stood outside the building. Not far from us, in fact. With an earnest look on his face, he was saying.

"The latest exclusive from KF5 news here at the office siege, is that the hostage taker has just released a set of demands. He is asking for the release of a number of prisoners, Separatist rebels currently serving time for various acts of terrorism. We will shortly be speaking to the local police here to get their reaction. In the meantime, it's back to Brad in the studio and our panel of experts."

"What the fuck?" I exclaimed and was about to call for Hendriksen when she appeared in the doorway.

"Yes, I know," she said. "And it's the first I've heard of it, too. He must have contacted the media direct. I'll speak to the press now, downplay it."

"So much for keeping it quiet." observed Pops. Then Javez spoke up.

"We're in, Skip."

I moved to look over her shoulder. From her monitor she was able to switch view from screen to screen inside the main office.

"Looks like six of them are still switched on." she said, working the keyboard.

"Good work. Is this two-way?"

"No, we can see in but they can't see out."

"Alright, keep on it, report every ten minutes, tell me what you can see."

In the meantime, some sandwiches and coffee arrived. I took the opportunity to gather the rest of the team round for a sitrep while we ate. Important stuff taken care of, I opened the floor up to suggestions. A frontal assault was obviously out of the question.

Without knowing where everyone was, a covert assault was almost as risky. Javez had been watching her monitor, munching away, but not much had been revealed. So far, she had seen three hostages moving past the screens. They seemed to be unharmed, though their hands were zip tied. She had been unable to get audio, so no sounds to help us.

It was Pops who came up with the idea. While I had been doing the rounds he had been chatting to some of the spectators along the cordon and had bumped into an old guy who turned out to be the caretaker. Pops nipped out to find him again and brought him back to the CV. There, once offered a coffee and a doughnut, the old boy gave us the lowdown on rear entrances to the place, how to get into the main heating room and all the little nooks and crannies that invariably exist in a typical government building. After taking all that in, Pops took me to one side.

"I've got an idea. Want to let me run with it? It will involve just me going in, I think I can get close to the guy."

I rubbed my chin. "Worse case scenario?"

"He shoots me and you have a spare seat on the way back. But listen, Doc worked up a sedative and I found this little toy in our kit. Looks like a pistol but it fires a needle. Not much of a range on it but if I can get close enough I can pop him with it and job done, no one hurt."

I thought it on for a bit. "Okay, Pops, you've got your

shot. Two conditions. One, Javez wires you up so we can see and hear what's going on. Two, the team are standing by to come in at the first sign of trouble."

Pops nodded and I continued. "One thing, though, what if he spots the gun?"

Pops grinned. "That's the beauty of the plan. I want him to see the gun, I'm going to hand it over to him."

Plan decided, we ran the team through the details and got everyone kitted up and in place. I told Hendriksen to keep her people back and to especially keep the media as far way as she could. Pops, meanwhile, had gone off and reappeared in the caretaker's long brown coat, clutching a broom.

Khan couldn't suppress a laugh. "You going to sweep him off his feet, then?"

Pops grinned then ambled off, calm as you like, down the side of the building, swinging the caretaker's ring of keys and whistling as he went. The rest of the team took up concealed positions close by the main entrance, while Javez and I monitored from the CV. We had a nice view from the button camera in Pops coat and the sound was coming through loud and clear.

We watched as he unlocked and went through the louvred metal door into the boiler room at the rear of the building. From there, he went up some steps and came out into a corridor, whistling all the way. He made his way towards the central office, doing a bit of sweeping here and there, hunching his shoulders and putting on a bit of a limp.

Javez shook her head. "He's really getting into this role, isn't he?"

Some minutes later, Pops was directly outside the main office. He stopped his whistling and, with broom still in hand, cried out "Hello! Hello?"

The office door bust open to reveal our target, assault rifle at the ready, sweaty, bug eyed. Looking, to be honest, like a sack of shit.

"Who are you? Get your hands up!" Kadis waved the gun at Pops.

"Sorry, son," Pops replied calmly. "I'm just the caretaker. I came in the back way, there's cleaning to be done and I need to empty the bins."

"Hands up, I said!" Kadis shouted, glancing from side to side down the corridor.

"I'm on my own, son." Pops said, leaning the broom against the wall and raising his hands.

Kadis looked uncertain then, gesturing with the gun again ordered "Get in the room! No sudden moves!"

Pops complied, hands above his head. As he moved, he slowly turned, giving us a view of the whole office. There were a number of figures slumped along one wall, all zip tied from the looks of it, watching fearfully as Kadis came back in. He motioned Pops over towards the group.

"Over there! Slow! Do you have anything on you?"

Pops moved, maintaining his hunch and limp. He turned towards Kadis.

"Matter of fact I do, son. Truth is, those cops outside gave me a gun, should I give it to you?"

Kadis nodded jerkily. "Yes, hand it over, handle first."

Javez piped up. "Target is now showing on one of the PC screens." She pressed a key and we got a split screen view, one from Pop's POV, the other from a computer monitor off to the side. Pops lowered his hands slowly and pulled aside the brown coat to reveal the handle of the pistol in his belt. With two fingers, he slowly reached in and withdrew the gun from his belt, carefully turning it to offer it up, handle first, to Kadis. The gunman lowered his AR slightly and reached with one hand to take the offered weapon. Just as his fingers touched the handle Pops, moving with the smoothness of a snake, flipped the gun round, firing a needle into Kadis' neck. WIthout pause, Pops dropped the handgun and neatly snatched the rifle out of the man's grip.

Kadis staggered back into a desk, hand reaching up in vain to the thin needle now embedded in his skin. He stared up as Pops closed in to check he wasn't going for any other weapons, then feebly grasped the brown coat, mouthing a few words before slowly sinking to the carpet, out like a light.

I hadn't realised I'd been holding my breath until everyone in the CV let out a sigh. Pops glanced at the computer screen and winked.

"Target neutralised. Send 'em in, Mike."

I got onto Hendriksen immediately and within seconds her police and med teams were rushing into the building. The media, noticing the sudden activity, made a beeline for the entrance, leading to a scrum of cameras. Pops, meanwhile, came out the way he went in, casually strolling back down the side of the building and back to the CV. He even still had the broom with him.

A couple of hours later, everything at the scene resolved and paperwork done, we were back on *Lady Luck* heading back to base. The team were in good spirits and I was glad our first op had been a success. I did have one question for Pops, though, which I put to him on the way back.

"When he grabbed you, just before he went out, he said something. What was it?"

Pops frowned. "Well, that was a bit odd. He said "My family, please protect my family." Any idea what that means?"

I shrugged. "Could be a money thing, he'd lost his job, maybe that's why he had a chip on his shoulder?"

Pops muttered an agreement and we settled in for the jump back home.

CHAPTER 10

OPERATION WOLFE

We arrived back home to find that some of the unit had been assigned another mission. Carswell had left a briefing telling me he was setting up Operation Wolfe, a surveillance job on a suspected Cartel outfit back on Earth. He'd called in Kaur, Tahir, Saltzmann, Devlin and Bahadur. The rest of us would be pulled in as and when necessary. That gave us some time to complete our renovation of the base and get our training regimes properly underway.

More kit had arrived while we'd been away too. Our Marines, now known as The Twins, had pulled some strings and effected delivery of Noonan's latest models. A batch of new C6 SMGs and a couple of the latest N4 Plasma Guns. Half the weight of the old model, the N4s packed a real punch at close range. The first one I tested on the range vapourised not only my target but the ones adjacent. Armstrong yelled and punched the air, McNulty grinned and said "I think we best adjust the beam width a touch, Skip."

A few days later I gave the team leave to go off-base to the local town. While I wanted us to keep a low profile, nothing draws attention more than a mystery. I briefed the team to go out in small groups, visit some bars and restaurants, relax, chat "security work" and generally be seen to be normal working joes. That all went well, apart from the incident with Schrader, absent when the rest of the teams returned. We eventually tracked him down to a local casino, not a high class establishment by any accounts. It seemed our flyboy had something of a gambling habit.

How he got it past the selection process, I don't know. In any case, I called him in for tea and biscuits, just to talk it over. He held his hands up quick enough and swore it wouldn't affect his work in any way. I took him at his word. How team members spent their money and what they did in their own time was none of my concern. But I made it clear that the merest hint of it impinging on operational work and my size nine would be halfway up his arse before he knew it. Schrader ginned and left, Kuruk squeezing past him in the doorway.

"What's up?" I asked.

"Just thought you'd like to know, Skip." he tilted the screen of his E-Pad towards me.

"Kadis, our hostage taker. Died of a heart attack the day after being taken into custody."

"A heart attack? A man in his mid-30's?"

"Thirty two, Skip. Unusual but not impossible. Think of the strain he must have been under."

"Strain, yes, but a heart attack? How did you find out about it, regular news?"

Kuruk shook his head. "No, Skip. Not seen any sign of it on the usual channels. I heard through a source back at HQ. Want me to dig a bit more?"

I rubbed my chin."Yep, if you wouldn't mind. And thanks for letting me know."

Kuruk gave me one of his almost-smiles and left. I settled back in my chair, parked my feet on the desk and, for the first time in months, relaxed.

I was woken by my E-pad's message tone. It was a summons from Carswell to bring the team in on Operation Wolfe. A Navy frigate, *Dolphin*, was en route to our system. We were to rendezvous with it in a couple of days time and it would carry us back to Earth. With a stretch and a sigh, I stood and sent a message out over the base coms system for everyone to assemble in the briefing room.

Schrader guided *Lady Luck* into the open belly of the frigate and, within minutes, the bay doors were sealed and Navy bods were showing us to our quarters. As we'd only be on board for a few days, we left our gear on the transport. Settled in, the call came over ship coms to prepare for jump. The gate in our system would take us directly to Sol, so just a short jump in the scheme of things. Me, I'd kind of gotten used to Inter Sysytem Jumps over the years. They never felt entirely natural. Going through a gate always gave you a vague sensation of dislocation, of something being wrong; there was always a vague feeling that the human body was not supposed to be travelling in this way. A Navy captain at an official do once explained to me how it worked. Something to do with the Murukami Drive utilising folds in space at a quantum level, or something. I'd just smiled and nodded politely while he spoke. I think he'd mistaken my interest in his First Officer for an interest in space travel. She took the opportunity to escape, so the interest obviously wasn't mutual.

Anyway, when it came to ISJs, most of the team took it the same way, apart from Haugen. The big man constantly grumbled into his beard and fidgeted in his nervousness. The Marines, being Navy, constantly ribbed him over it.

We entered the Sol system via the Jupiter Gate and a call came over the tannoy, "All stations, prepare for Earth approach."

The team were gathering personal effects together in readiness to head down to the bay, when a Naval rating popped her head round the door to inform me that the Captain had invited me up to the bridge. I followed her through the narrow corridor to a lift and, minutes later, the doors hissed open to reveal the main bridge. A pair of Marines flanked the doorway, like statues. In contrast, the rest of the place was a hive of activity. A tall, lean, olive-skinned figure with thinning hair rose from the Captain's chair to greet me with a salute and a firm handshake.

"Rahal," he smiled. "Sorry I never came down to see you earlier. We've been running some training exercises while on en route, you know how it is."

I returned the smile. "Naylor. Yes, I do. Never ending, isn't it?"

He smiled. "I don't know if this is your first visit to Earth but I thought you might like to see the old place as we come in. It's a view I never get tired of."

Rahal turned and gestured to the large viewscreen. It was the first time I'd actually seen Earth. On my last visit, I was tucked away like a piece of baggage. Seeing that blue orb hanging in the darkness of space brought a strange feeling in my gut. I suppose you could call it nostalgia, though for what I'm not sure. I guess all of us, in some way, see coming to Earth as returning home, even though we're Offworlders. The orb slowly grew until it filled most of the view screen and I could make out the shapes of continents beneath the clouds. Then the view abruptly changed to a beaming, smiling face sat beneath a bright orange turban.

"Ahoy, ANV *Dolphin.* This is Orbital Control, please respond, over."

The Captain responded. "Roger, Orbital Control, this is ANV *Dolphin.* Acknowledged, over".

"Thank you *Dolphin.* Please maintain position. A guide shuttle will be with you in two minutes to take you into Orbital Dock Five, over and out."

There was a sudden disappearance of the low level hum that I hadn't even realised was there, as the main engines were shut down, followed by an odd sensation of stillness. The guide shuttle appeared and the bridge crew went smoothly about their tasks, piloting the vessel towards the looming space dock that was locked into orbit above the North American continent. Transports of every type came and went every few minutes, larger vessels moved out beyond us towards the Sol gates.

The frigate was guided with precision into a large, gantry type structure and there was a slight clunk and shudder as the ship was docked. The crew immediately seemed to relax and excited chatter broke out across the bridge. Rahal smiled again.

"They're looking forward to shore leave, we've been out for three months. Anyway, welcome to Earth, I hope your stay is a pleasant one."

I shook the Captain's hand and thanked him for a smooth trip, then took the lift down to the bay to meet the rest of the team at our transport. Everything and everyone was stowed aboard and within minutes we dropped out of the open bay doors and Schrader pointed our nose Earthwards. The heat shields obscured the view as we entered the atmosphere but, once they lifted, we had the glorious sight of the American continent spread out beneath us.

We were landing in Canada, again. Not at CIHQ this time but at the nearby Kingston Military Base. Once boots touched ground, we were assigned a private barracks block, guarded by the local troops. A grinning Kaur was waiting for us. Some hot food arrived and, as we nosebagged, she filled us in with a sitrep.

The target was a Cartel drugs factory situated over the border, near a place called Boston. Kaur forwarded local maps to our E- pads as she explained the job.

"The factory is situated in what used to be a large industrial estate. I've established an OPS about twenty klicks north of Boston, close enough for access, far enough out to not be seen."   She highlighted a spot on the map.

"There's have a hover waiting for us when you're ready to move out, Skip. Thought it would be best if we hitched a lift with the locals. They know the territory."

I nodded my thanks and we set about transferring our gear over to the hover. I asked Pops to stay behind to act as liaison with the locals. Schrader was stay behind too, ready to fly *Lady Luck* in at short notice should we need her.

The hover was cramped, what with all of us and our kit. Before we boarded Kaur gave each of us an adhesive, bright green patch to stick on our upper arms.

"Radiation monitors," she explained. "While it's green, it's okay. If the radiation level changes, it darkens to red, then blue."

"Radiation?" asked Wiz.

Kuruk interjected. "The war. The strike on Boston was a low-yield bomb, according to the records. Any residual effects should be long gone by now but it's probably best to be safe rather than sorry."

"In other words, don't drink the water!" grinned Kaur. "Oh, and best avoid contact with the local civs as well, they aren't the welcoming types for the most part."

The pilot and co-pilot were already in place, and we were soon up and heading south across a large lake. The co-pilot, Rogers, according to his name tag, turned in his seat.

"Below us you can see Lake Ontario. During and after the war, a lot of people tried to come across the lake into Canada. These days it's much quieter. We mostly patrol for jib smugglers or people traffickers."

"Jib? What's jib" asked Armstrong.

"Drugs. We have quite a problem with runners from over the border. They supply the criminal gangs working the cities."

Once across the lake, the nose of the hover turned south-east and we began to cross over heavily forested terrain. The pilot took us up a little higher, then dipped a wing. The co-pilot turned again.

"If you look out to starboard, you can just make out New York in the distance."

Those of us on that side of the craft peered out. In the far haze, I could just make out the shapes of tall buildings; they looked jagged and broken.

"New York was hit as well as Boston," explained Kuruk. "Must have been terrible. So many killed, so many refugees."

Rogers nodded. "Yeah, it was a serious problem at one

time. Hundreds of thousands headed north to get into Canada, it was overwhelming. In the end, the government built a wall along part of the border to try and keep things under control. They were worried about the spread of radiation- related sickness, I guess."

"What's it like these days?" asked McNulty.

The co-pilot shrugged. "Like I said before, along the border its quiet for the most part. We don't normally head out this far. If you keep an eye out, below you'll see the occasional fortified community. That's how the population here lives now. Then there's the travelling groups, bands of outlaws and scavengers for the most part. The big cities are in ruins."

"Is there no local law and order? No military presence?" said Haugen.

"None to speak of," answered Rogers. "The poor sods down there have to fend for themselves, eh?"

"No back up for us, then?" Haugen scowled.

"Well, we have orders to be on stand-by. If we get the call, we can shift a couple of platoons across within the hour, long as it ain't weatherin."

The hover next nudged east and soon the remains of Boston could be seen ahead. A dark smudge on the horizon resolved into another collection of ruined skyscrapers. Beyond lay the grey Atlantic. Our craft put in a turn and began to descend. Minutes later, we touched down onto an open tarmac area; an old school, Kaur explained.

We disembarked to find Tahir and Saltzmann waiting for us with a couple of civvie vehicles. I had a quick shufty around the place while the gear was being transferred. At the edge of the tarmac was a long, low building. The school I guess. It was a shell; empty windows, roof collapsed in places. At the front, I found a wooden board half hanging off a post, partly covered in weeds. I could make out the words WELC T ARKH IGH OOL.

Beyond lay empty streets, overgrown with weeds, the only noise the squeak of a rusty sign swinging in the breeze. The weather was cool, the sky overcast and grey, the shadows lengthening as the sun went down. I thought I could detect a faint tang of sea on the air. My daydream was interrupted by Tahir.

"We're ready to roll, Skip. It's not far."

Over her shoulder I could see the hover lift off, turn, then disappear into the deepening twilight gloom. I jumped aboard one of the trucks and, after a five minute drive through deserted streets, we were at Kaur's OPS. She had chosen well. An old apartment building set up on a ridge on the edge of town. There was an open view of Boston to the south and good coverage of all the approach roads. The trucks were locked away in the garage underneath the building. We settled in, then gathered for another briefing session.

In the meantime, I'd had some more intel come through from Carswell which I relayed to the team. We had a man on the inside, it seemed, a low level Cartel man looking to turn. It was he who had first blown the whistle on the location of the factory. I flashed his mug up on the screen.

"So, this is Max Savik. Low level Cartel enforcer."

"Pretty, ain't he?" chuckled Armstrong. I had to admit Max was no looker; squat, bald, a livid scar down one cheek. Still, he was our man for this job and we were under strict orders to bring him in unharmed. That out of the way, Tahir took over to bring us up to speed, showing where the team had established OP's around the target. Devlin and Bahadur were still out in the field. They had a couple of hides up on the wooded hills overlooking the industrial estate. Tahir pulled up maps and ran the drone footage the team had collected over the last few weeks.

"As you can see, the place has been well chosen. It's out of the way, difficult to approach without being seen and tucked away in a tangle of old plants and factories."

Tucked away was the word. The target buildings were centred in a compound that itself lay in the heart of the industrial area.

McNulty raised his hand. "No chance of local help then, or a major assault?"

"Depends on what plans we come up with". I replied. "Carswell has let me know he can send down some troops from the north if we need them. But there isn't the manpower or the willpower for a full on assault."

"It would be difficult tactically, too," added Koenig studying the maps. "Any large force would be seen coming in from some distance, air or ground, especially if Tango has spotters up on those hills."

Tahir nodded. "We can't discount the fact that the Cartel may have eyes and ears amongst the locals."

"Plus," added Koenig, "that place would be a nightmare to assault. It looks like a maze. FIB always favours the defending force."

I nodded. "So a low key assault looks the most likely. Once in, we call for back up and the cavalry will come riding in?"

Armstrong shrugged. "Why not just bomb the place? It's not like there's any real estate to be damaged, is there?"

"True, but there is another problem." Kaur took a sip of coffee and extracted a large photo from her sheaf of papers. "According to our inside man, the Cartel are using civvie workers in various roles in their operation. They have shipped in a few high level chemists and are holding their families at the factory. In effect, they are hostages."

"How about a drop, Skip?" asked Chen.

I had to smile. The Marines wanted to bomb the place, the Landers wanted to drop on it. Kaur stepped in. "A suit drop might be possible, it would have to be very accurate. But it would take time to set up and would involve more people. A chute drop, probably not so feasible. We are on the coast and weather conditions can change rapidly."

Koenig nudged Tahir. "Can you run through that drone footage again, about three minutes in." Tahir complied and Koenig asked her to freeze the frame.

"There." He strode up to the screen and pointed. "The main gate. We send a team in through the main gate, it's the only way in and out. Meanwhile, other teams move in from the perimeter, here, here and... here. See? These approaches have plenty of cover from the other buildings. As soon as we are in, the back up lands to seal the place off.

"What's on the perimeter?" I asked.

Kaur answered "The place is bordered by a standard wire fence. No sentries around it, though according to Devlin, they conduct occasional patrols of the surrounding area."

"How do the patrols go out? On foot or vehicles?" asked Koenig.

Kaur checked through her notes. "Vehicle. An APC,

normally, with a group of three or four in it"

"And what numbers are we looking at inside?"

Tahir checked her screen. "According to Pretty Boy, there are three boffins with five assistants who are the brains of the operation. The actual manufacturing is carried out by fifteen workers, some drawn from the hostage families. There's Max and another enforcer overseeing, backed up by a dozen goons."

"All armed, I presume?"

"Yes Skip. The Cartel is rich enough to buy decent hardware. We can presume they have state of the art security and surveillance too. However, the fact they are so tucked away and think nobody knows they are there may make them lax."

"Supplies? Back up?" asked Kuruk.

Kaur took over again."Supplies are dropped in by hover once a month. They have the APC and a couple of other vehicles on the ground, that's it."

"Okay," I stood up. "The APC looks the best bet. Let's sort a plan to grab it, then use it as our key to the door. As it goes in we'll have two other teams work in from the perimeter. Let's keep the Canadians on call, I want them in as quick as possible once we're moving. Devlin can be set in place in advance to lend sniper support. Doc and Wiz, I want you to lead a group to sort out the families, get them out of there as quick as you can."

Doc nodded. "We'll need extra transport for them, Skip. Ask the locals to send an extra transport over, too."

"Good thinking, Doc." I checked the time. "Tahir, can you call Devlin and Bahadur? Arrange an RV with them tomorrow. Alright everyone, let's get some rest and reconvene at 0600."

By noon the next day, I was squashed into a hide alongside Devlin overlooking the main road into the industrial estate. Everything was still and quiet, it was a pleasant day with sunshine and birdsong. It was nice to know that not everything had been wiped out in the war.

"The APC is due out tomorrow," Devlin said, sweeping the area before us with his binos. " T h e y normally go out once a week. They work up this main road then make a circuit up that hill, there's a large track running along the top. Then they drop back down over there." He motioned with his hand and I followed his gesture with my binos. "Through that wood, then they swing up onto the road to the south, which brings them back round to the front here."

I thought for a moment. "The woods is where we hit them. Then we use the APC to go in the front door, the rest of us come through the fence. Can you infil into the estate tonight and find a good fire position?"

Devlin nodded and I left him to it, jogging back to our

truck parked up under cover on the reverse side of the hill. Douglas was sat in the driving seat and, once I told him the plan, he suggested making up some small charges that could be used to blow the wire fence. Once back at the CP, we refined the details and checked weapons and equipment. Kuruk was to stay at the CP, the rest of us were going to move out pre-dawn to take up positions. McNulty and Koenig were leading the fence assault teams, I was leading the APC team, consisting of Tahir, Armstrong, Slade and Chen. Doc was to move in right behind us with Wiz, Mir and Vitali. Abomo was stationed up on the hill supervising the comsnet and keeping in touch with Schrader back at the Canuck base.

Things started off well. Tucked away in the woods, my team got the signal from Abomo that the APC had just come out of the complex. That gave us around twenty minutes. With a final tightening of bongos and ammo checks, we took up position. Sure enough, we soon heard the hum of the engine approaching. From concealment, I watched as the squat shape appeared at the top of the rise, before dipping down into the track running through the glade. The plan was simple, a felled tree would stop the vehicle, someone would get out to investigate, bang, we're in. I should have learnt by now that no plan survives contact with the enemy.

The APC came up to our felled tree but no one got out.

Instead, the goon inside decided to try and nudge the tree out of the way. He did a good job, too. The tree was shifting bit by bit, soon the track would be clear. So I made a command decision.

Swearing, I left cover and ran in a crouch to the rear of the APC. Once there, I hammered on the door, hoping someone might open up, I suppose. The door didn't open but the hatch on top did and a blond head popped out. He clocked me and shouted back down inside the vehicle. Then he made his fatal mistake. Rather than pop back in, he reached down and came out with a handful of pistol, which he pointed in my direction. There was a crack from the undergrowth and his head disappeared in a red spray, his lifeless body falling back into the APC. That did it. The engine gunned and, with a last effort, our makeshift barricade was shoved aside. Now it became a case of not capturing the vehicle but stopping it.

I shouted out "Disable it! Disable it!" and Armstrong came charging out of the undergrowth, fiddling with the mechanism on the plasma gun. He braced, took aim and let fly a bolt of shimmering white-blue energy. There was an almighty bang as the APC disintegrated in a blinding flash. The air crackled and was filled with sizzling shrapnel. I picked myself up off the ground. Armstrong stood slack-jawed. All that remained of the APC was a large scorch mark on the ground and a circle of fragments, none larger than a fist.

Slade was doubled over with laughter. Between fits, he pointed at Armstrong and said, "You were only supposed to blow the bloody doors off!"

I didn't have a clue what he meant, but I wasn't in the mood for laughing. I thought fast and called up the other teams. We would need to move sharpish before the patrol was missed, so I decided we would roll up in our truck and play it by ear. Risky but Landers thrive on risk.

Fifteen minutes later, we were rolling along the highway in our truck. It was civvie, no markings and as we drove I was wracking my brains for a story to tell the goons at the gate. We came to the outskirts of the industrial area and I slowed down, following the signs to the chemical plant. A few turns and there it was, an access road off the main way leading to the entrance.

The gates were open but there was a barrier blocking the way, next to a sentry booth. It looked to be manned by two or three goons. There was no chance of crashing the barrier and I still had no real plan. While the goons were in the booth they could presumably get a signal off to the gang inside. But how to get them out into the open?

Tahir, in the passenger seat, said to me, "Slow down!" and began wriggling out of her webbing.

"Stop here!" she said as we were about five metres away from the gate. "Be ready to move on my signal!" she grinned before slipping out of the cab and heading towards the sentry post. She had removed her gear and let down her long, black hair. She carried no weapons, though it looked like had something in her hand behind her back. As she walked forward, she undid a few buttons on her top and affected what I can only describe as a sashaying walk. She strolled right up to the booth and tapped on the window, calling "Hello! I seem to be lost, can you help me?"

I could make out the grinning face of the goon inside as he reached forward and slid open the booth window. Without a pause, Tahir dropped the grenade she had been carrying in through the opening and shouted "Go!".

The team were out of the truck and sprinting forward in a flash, as three figures came bursting out of the booth. Tahir tripped one and Armstrong was on him immediately. Slade shot off like a rocket and tackled the second, he hit the tarmac with a grunt. The third was light on his heels though, he was off and sprinting towards the main building like shit off a shovel. Chen raised his assault rifle and took careful aim but, before he could fire, there was a faint crack and the goon went down pole-axed. Another strike for Devlin!

I shouted into the comsnet, "Go! Go! Go!". Almost immediately, there were crumps from the near distance as the fences were blown. Tahir already had the two guards cuffed and Slade raised the barrier as I rolled the truck in. Jumping out, AK at the ready, I joined the team as they advanced in assault formation, scanning nearby doors and windows.

One doorway opened, framing a Cartel man who snatched at his waist for a pistol. Chen's burst took him in the chest and he wheeled and fell back into the interior. I waved Chen over and he and Armstrong headed for the door, throwing in a flash grenade before disappearing inside.

A shot whistled past my head from above. I instantly turned and sprayed an upper window. Glass shattered as a figure disappeared from view. I heard more gunfire from ahead and the thump of a grenade. Armstrong and Chen popped back out of the doorway, signalling all clear.

We focused ahead on the main entrance to the factory building itself. I nodded and Chen kicked the door in, crouched, SMG at the ready. There was no response so we entered quickly, each covering a separate arc of fire with our weapons. More gunfire, followed by shouts, sounded from ahead, then a figure came racing towards us, another Cartel goon. On seeing me, he shouted an expletive and raised his weapon. He was immediately cut down by the fire of our three guns.

Within five minutes we had linked up with Koenig's team and had the main building secured. The second team were mopping up the rest of the compound. Doc had followed us in on the other truck and was seeing to the hostage families; they looked in a right state. The remaining goons were soon rounded up and disarmed. Haugen was covering them as they knelt, hands on heads, on the tarmac at the front of the building. Max was among them, eyeing us nervously. We'd been told not to blow his cover so we had to treat him the same as the rest. Kaur was leading some equally nervous looking science types out, blinking, into the daylight.

I gave the all clear to Abomo, who told me Schrader and our back-up were already on the way. Sure enough, within about thirty minutes, the shadow of our transport fell over the compound, followed by a group of hovers. They landed in a nice square formation, surrounding an unmarked hover that landed in the centre. Troops piled out of the four, forming a protective cordon around the central vehicle, from which two figures emerged, both civvies from the look of it. All very impressive but totally unnecessary. Haugen looked up from guarding the prisoners and laughed.

"Who the fuck are these guys?"

The two suits strode over, escorted by a group of soldiers who were dramatically sweeping their AR's around to cover the surrounding area. The lead figure was a tall man in his 60's, white hair swept back in an impressive coiffure. His colleague was a short, rotund figure, slightly boggle eyed, who immediately put me in mind of a frog. The tall one headed straight for me.

"You must be Naylor?"

I nodded. "I am. And this area is secured, you can tell your people to stop waving their guns around."

The man sniffed. "My name is Reynolds, I am assuming control of this operation. Your people are to vacate immediately. If you check your E-pad, I think you will find confirmation orders from your superior."

I made to reply but the man had already turned and was striding off into the factory, his squat assistant following. Charmed, I'm sure. I checked my E-pad and, sure enough, there was a message from Carswell. That was that, then. I rounded up the team and told them to assemble over by *Lady Luck*; Schrader had landed her back out on the main road.

I got over there, took off my helmet and lit up a syg while I waited for the others. The sun was hot on my face and I sat on the warm tarmac, my back against the landing gear and took a deep breath. The usual post-op comedown. From briefing to execution, you are all fired up. You can be running on adrenalin for hours, then, suddenly, it's all finished. If you're lucky, you are still in one piece. Even so, any nerves you pushed aside can now come back with a vengeance if you are not careful.

Everyone gradually appeared, a grimacing Chen, one trouser leg ripped and torn, supported by Koenig and Williams.

"Just a flesh wound," grinned Koenig. "He got skimmed on the way in."

I shook my head, smiling. "Don't you ever get tired of getting holes in your shirt, Chen?"

Chen smiled back. "Don't you know chicks dig scars, Skip?"

Doc, having finished with the hostages, was fussing over Jacobs as they walked over.

I stood up, asking, "You okay?"

She sighed. "Just some cuts from flying glass, Skip, nothing serious."

I glanced at Doc, who nodded and continued cleaning up Jacobs' face.

Soon, everyone was back. I noticed Wiz off away from the group, chatting to Tahir. She looked shaken. I gave them a few minutes, then walked over. Tahir was trembling, her eyes were teared up.

"You alright, T?" I asked.

She nodded. Wiz turned to me. "Nothing to worry about, Skip. That was her first major fire-fight. Comes as a bit of a shock, eh?"

Tahir wiped the back of her hand across her eyes. "Yep, it certainly does."

I smiled and squeezed her arm. "Don't worry, it gets easier. And that was good work you did at the gatepost. Quick thinking! Now, soldier, I want you ready to fly out in five, got it?"

Tahir coughed and smiled. "Got it, Skip."

I turned back to see a beaming Pops stick his head out of the transport door.

"Hello, playmates," he laughed. "I bring coffee and hot scran."

Sure enough, there was a waft of coffee floating out the hatchway. Just then, a horn sounded behind us as Kuruk rolled up in our other truck, with Abomo and the rest of our gear on board. Twenty minutes later, we were airborne once more.

Carswell was waiting for us back at the Canadian base. He was all smiles, the higher ups were happy with us, it seemed. So much so, that we were to be given four days leave here on Earth. Better still, a flight had been arranged for us to visit a smart holiday resort in Barbados, which turned out to be a very nice tropical island. I did ask the Chief who the double act at the plant where, he merely said, "Need to know, Naylor, need to know."

Anyway, as twenty four hours later I was sat on a warm beach sipping an ice cold beer, I let it slip.

CHAPTER 11

THE SIEGE

One thing you soon learn in the services is that nothing good ever lasts. We were only two days into our leave when the call came through. To make matters worse, it was early morning, and an early morning after a full-on night before at that. We may be able to hurl a spaceship between solar systems but science still hasn't come up with a decent hangover cure. Bleary-eyed, head pounding, I took the call from Carswell and put out the call for everyone to meet at the bar by the pool. I bumped into Kaur and Pops in the hotel corridor on the way there.

"What is it, Skip?" asked Kaur, her mirror shades reflecting my pale face.

"Don't know yet. The Chief just said there's a developing situation and we're on stand-by."

Schrader had already organised a hair of the dog and full breakfast. Once the whole team had gathered, I suggested we polish the grub off sharpish then get prepared to move out.

"No rest for the wicked, eh?" grumbled Haugen, before enthusiastically diving into the plate of greasy food before him. My stomach flipped at the sight and I settled for a glass of fizzy water instead.

An hour later we were in the air, heading for Switzerland. The full sitrep was coming in from Carswell. I piped him over the intercom so everyone could hear.

"It's the concert hall at Lucerne. A team of terrorists infiltrated the audience at last night's concert. They are all armed and may possibly be carrying or wearing explosives. We're not sure who they are at the moment, or what they want but they are holding around eight hundred people hostage, a number of leading politicians and other high flyers amongst them. On landing you are to report to and liaise with General Charbonnier of European Command. He's heading the operation on the ground. All current info being forwarded now ."

"Roger, Chief. Over and out."

Kuruk was already researching, pulling up info on the concert hall, sourcing news broadcasts and linking into the CIS mainframe. We had a few hours of flying ahead so I let him get on with it and shut my eyes for a nap, my head was still pounding.

Kaur shook me awake and motioned out of the window.

"Sunset over the Alps," she said.

It certainly was a majestic site and I was able to appreciate it even more as my headache had faded. Not long after, we touched down at the local airport and were met by a military police team who drove us off to Charbonnier's CP.

This guy had style, he was shacked up in a very smart local hotel. In fact, the whole town looked very upmarket, way above my pay grade. We were greeted by the General's aide, who asked if there was anything we needed.

"Some coats would be great, please! It's freezing here and we've just come from the Bahamas!" Kaur immediately said.

The aide laughed and said he would see to it, as the General himself came in. I took to him straight away. He had a no nonsense look about him, a compact, keen eyed man who moved with easy grace. Neatly turned out, but with a constant syg on the go, he greeted us in accented English and invited us into his room for a briefing. There were only the three of us; Kaur, myself and Kuruk. I'd left the rest to sort out quarters and set up our own OPS.

The situation was bad. A performance had just started of some old, classical music, when a group of around thirty to forty masked and heavily armed figures burst into the concert hall lobby and began firing AR's into the air. Within minutes, they had taken control of the building and sealed off the audience and performers inside. There was very little local security, we were presuming that any guards inside had been overwhelmed. The local plod had the area locked-down quick sharp and the military were called in. Various intel agencies were also on the case, I gather there had been some kind of inter-departmental wrangling over who exactly was in charge, par for the course with REMFs.

The General confirmed Carswell's info that many of the concert-goers were high flyers. I guess you had to be to live round here or to visit this kind of place. So far, there had been no word from the terrorists other than a brief cam transmission to say they had total control of the building and any sign of interference would lead to hostages being killed. Suddenly the General's aide burst into the room, looking flustered, closely followed by a detachment of smart-suited close protection types, who swept in and began scanning everyone and everything for weapons.

The General had just started demanding to know what the hell was going on when a further two CP bods swept in, flanking a smartly dressed, dark haired woman in her late fifties. Her green eyes took in the whole the room, not missing a thing, her face breaking into a beaming smile on seeing Pops.

"Gervaise!" she beamed and strode over to shake

Pops' hand. "So nice to see you again!"

He returned the smile and handshake with a small bow of his head.

"Madame President," he said. "Nice to see you too, I trust you are well?"

By now, the General was standing to ramrod attention as introductions were made. This was the closest I'd been to a real life leader. President Theodorou had been Head of the Senate for the last four years and she had a reputation as a shrewd operator and a tough cookie, standing up to the corporations on more than one occasion. She certainly had a good grasp on the situation here and picked the General up immediately on several minor details. As the two were in a serious head-to-head, I took the opportunity to sidle over to Pops and whispered to him with a grin.

"Gervaise? I never knew your first name was Gervaise."

Pops whispered back, the smile on his face not flickering for an instant, "You ever tell anyone…. *anyone*… and I'll break both your arms."

I chuckled, then straightened up as La Presidente and the General finished their conflab. Another sweep of bodyguards and she was gone, off to a press conference according to Charbonne. He informed us of the time and place of the next OB and, with that we were shown out and left to find our comrades.

Carswell called in later that night to inform me that AT5's role here was purely consultative unless further orders came through. That made clear, I assigned Kuruk, Pops, Mir and Abomo direct to the General and kept the rest of the team on full alert, ready to move at a moment's notice.

As it turned out, nothing much happened for the next three days. Mir and Abomo supervised the attempted surveillance of the concert hall interior. Built at the turn of the 21st century, the place was a complex of halls and theatres rather than a single building and that worked for and against us. To one side, lay a tangle of old buildings and a maze of narrow streets. Setting up an OP was no problem. On the other side, the complex lay on the shoreline of a large lake. That cut down on options for approach but did also narrow down avenues of escape, nothing could get across the lake without being seen. Checking the building plans, we did find that various waterways led to and from the lake into the building itself, giving us at least one good option for infil.

In the meantime, the terrorists had released a statement to the press, beaming it direct to various global news agencies. They claimed to be part of a Spart group and were demanding withdrawal of TA forces from a number of Rim planets and the release of a number of prisoners. Failure to do so would result in the deaths of all the hostages, they said. The Sparts also made it clear they had no qualms about giving up their own lives and even showed briefly on the cam link how the interior of the hall had been rigged with explosives.

Food and drink had been delivered on a daily basis, as per the Sparts' demands. At this stage, the General's strategy was to go along with the situation, buying time while a rescue plan could be formulated. The higher-ups weren't happy that the Sparts could speak directly to the media, so Mir was put on the case to block any unauthorised in or out-going coms.

It was on the fourth day that a plan was finalised. I'd been invited to the OB and sat round an impressive antique table with over a dozen others, each representing a different agency. The bad news was that amongst them was a spook from the Department of Internal Security. These guys were a law unto themselves, they even made the regular Green Slime look reasonable. Everyone knew of them but no one knew much about them. Pops had told me that following a heated discussion in the The Senate, the DIS had recently had their funding and powers increased. In certain circumstances, they now had powers of command over any regular forces units which was bound to be an unpopular move. It was them who put forward the rescue plan.

Once prelims had been gotten out of the way, the DIS man, who to me had the looks, bearing and charm of a vulture, stood to speak. He introduced himself as simply *Pisani, DIS* and informed the group about a new toxin that had been developed. This was an odourless, colourless gas that would totally incapacitate the central nervous system within a matter of seconds. The plan was simple, pump the gas into the hall, count to five, then send in masked up teams to neutralise the Sparts. Med units would then move in to medevac the hostages and administer an antidote to the toxin.

Questions were asked about this wonder gas but Pisani assured all present that it would be not only effective but safe for all concerned. That decided, details were drawn up for both delivering the gas and organising the assault teams. It was planned to go in early morning hours, before daylight. The power to the complex would also be cut, while our teams would have NVGs.

Kuruk put forward the notion of leaking a false time to the terrorists, giving the impression we were going in a few hours earlier. It was a good idea, the Sparts would be on high alert for a while then, when nothing happened, they'd naturally relax. Kick off was set for 0500 a day later, which gave over 24 hours to get everything in place. Pisani informed us that the toxin was already close to hand, being held in an unmarked tanker outside of the city limits with a team of specialist engineers attached. That settled, everyone went their own ways to begin preparations.

I didn't have much to do, not being directly involved in the assault. Mir and Abomo continued as part of the surveillance team and the General drafted in Vitali, Bahadur, Khan, Williams and Koenig to oversee final prep of the assault teams. Doc, Wiz and Jacobs volunteered to go in with the meds to assist.

I had a good view as the operation unfolded, being present in the main control centre, watching events as they happened via our surveillance devices and the assault teams' body cams. The early stages went like a dream. The gas was pumped in, people started falling and the teams made their move. There was a brief firefight in the lobby, with three Sparts shot for one of ours but the rest of the place was sleeping like babies. The teams quickly moved throughout the building to secure it, while all exits and entrances were covered from outside. Then came the first hiccup. Once the building was secured, Pisani took the coms and made the announcement.

"All terrorists are to be terminated immediately!"

The General looked shocked, this wasn't something that had been discussed at the briefing. I imagine it was planned that the Sparts would be taken prisoner for questioning and imprisonment. The General said as much but the DIS man dismissed his protests with a shrug.

"We must send a clear message, General," he explained. "These rebels must learn that the price of attacking the Alliance is their total destruction."

"I'll not order my personnel to shoot helpless people, Sparts or not!" The General responded but it was already too late. The DIS team that had overseen the pumping of the gas were now moving through the hall, shooting with pistols each and every Spart they found. Koenig's voice flashed up in my personal earpiece.

"Skip, are you seeing this?"

I moved away from the command group and responded.

"I see it, Koenig. DIS orders."

"Fuckers!" Williams' voice piped in too. My response was cut short by a call from Doc.

"Skip, we have a problem. Jacobs is down!"

"What happened, Doc, is she hit?"

"Negative. Looks like an equipment malfunction. Overcome by the gas, I think. Am arranging medevac for her now."

"Thanks, Doc, keep me posted."

"Want some more bad news, Skip?" This time it was Khan.

I groaned. "Not really, but go on."

"Bahadur is hurt. We were rappelling down and his rope snapped. Twenty metre drop to the floor. Bad case of RDS, he's being carried out now."

"Shit. Okay, Kahn, do me a favour, go with him will you? Report back when you know more."

I turned back to the command group. Things looked tense. The General was on the blower to someone and, from his expression, he was being put in his place. Pisani was doing his best not to look smug, but failing. Meanwhile on the screens, med vehicles were now swarming around the exterior of the complex and unconscious hostages were being carried out. I figured there was nothing I could do here, so I returned to our quarters to let the rest of the team know what was happening.

It was a few hours later that I got called up to the de-brief. Pisani had disappeared, the General was pacing up and down the room in a fury. I'd had news from Khan that Bahadur had shattered both legs and was undergoing surgery, so I was not in the best of moods myself. That worsened when I heard what the General had to say.

"Over eighty hostages dead and many more still unconscious! Plus a dozen of our own troops still suffering the effects of the gas!" He swore in a foreign language. "They said this gas was safe to use! Losing people in action is one thing but this is bullshit. Where the hell is Pisani?"

The General's aide piped up. "We don't know, sir. He and his team are no longer on site. Last we heard, they were seen heading towards the airport."

At that moment, Doc entered and caught my eye.

"Skip. They said you were here. I've just come from the hospital. Jacobs didn't make it. She passed away thirty minutes ago, she never came round from the gas."

I clenched my fists and took a breath. "How come she was gassed?"

Doc shook her head angrily. "Seems that some of the equipment issued was faulty. Her respirator malfunctioned. Not just her's, there are others, too."

"Yes, the General was just saying. But I thought they had an antidote to the toxin?"

"Preliminary observations would suggest that the antidote is only around 75% effective," replied Doc.

"For fuck's sake!" I banged my fist on the table.

"There's something else, Skip. Remember that funny frog looking man who turned up at the drugs factory? Well, I swear I saw him at the hospital talking to some of the higher-ups."

"Okay, Doc, thanks. Listen, get yourself some grub and grab some rest. Tell the team I'll be back once I've finished here. I'll be glad to get out and way from this mess."

CHAPTER 12

UTOPIS

Twenty four hours later, we were back on *Lady Luck* and heading off-world. We had Bahadur with us, mildly sedated but stable. There was no way we were leaving anyone behind, besides which we had enough facilities to look after him ourselves. Jacobs was with us, too. The unit formed an honour guard as her coffin was carried on board. She had no known family, so she would travel back to base with us and be interred there. Like I said, we don't like to leave anyone behind.

The mood on board was sombre as we broke atmosphere to rendezvous with the frigate *Poseidon*. Carswell had been in contact to express his condolences at our loss and to pass on thanks from Charbonnier for our part in the mission. He suggested that as our leave had been interrupted, I give the team a few more days' break before heading back to base. I talked it over with the frigate Captain, name of Wright. She suggested a stay at *Utopis*, an orbital leisure facility that sat close to Space Way Statopn 10 in the Hoyle System. The frigate was passing through the system, so it seemed like a no-brainer. I spread the good news amongst the team. Little did I know that even more trouble was waiting in store.

We had just entered the system and were gathering all our shit together when Kuruk tapped me on the shoulder.

"Skip, I think you should take a look it this."

Flipping round his E-pad he began showing me a bunch of media reports concerning the siege operation. None of them was good. The basic headline and story in each was how the spec ops units had made a complete mess of the assault and how scores of innocent people had died as a result. No mention of any gas and certainly no mention of DIS.

I kicked the bulkhead. "Arseholes!"

"There's more, Skip." Kuruk glanced around, then lowered his voice. "Back at that Cartel place, while you were all loading up, I had a quick look around. I managed to get a few pics and speak to some of the hostages. Turns out it wasn't a drugs factory... they were working on nerve toxins."

"What? So who else knew about this?"

"I don't know. I got spotted and chased out under the order of some civvie."

"Tall guy, white hair? Name of Reynolds, I think?"

"That's him. Anyway, I managed to get a snap of him, too, and have been following up some enquiries. Turns out he is a high-up in the Noonan Corporation, something to do with R&D. That's all I could discover. Information is scarce and hard to come by. Thought you'd like to know."

"Good work. Any more news on the Hirayama 5 guy?"

"Kadis? Not yet, but I have a couple of associates working on it."

Just then the intercom sounded, informing us that we should report to the landing bay for departure. Captain Wright told me that *Poseidon* had some local duties to carry out in the system and she would be back to pick us up in three days. Bahadur remained on board, in sick bay. He was recovering well from his surgery but was not likely to be up and mobile for quite some time yet. His main concern was that he would be off the team. I told him I'd do my best to keep him. In any case, I couldn't make any decision until the full med reports had come through.

Lady Luck dropped out the back of the frigate and turned ninety degrees, bringing *Utopis* into view. The lights of SWS10 twinkled beyond it, below we could see the red planet they both orbited. I'd briefly visited the place once before, some years back ,and it was apparent that it had lost none of its tacky charm.

The huge station was a kind of floating pleasure palace, casino and God knows what else. Most rumours had it being run by the Cartel. Not my ideal choice of leave venue but I figured the team could blow off some steam here for a few days. Schrader had called ahead to make all the arrangements; I might have know that he was all too familiar with the place. So, like a stern parent, I briefed them all at the boarding lock to have a good time but to behave! I should've known better.

Once we'd stowed gear in our rooms - Schrader had actually booked top of the line apartments for us, well, Carswell was paying - we hit the main strip to check out the bars and clubs. The place was built on four main levels. Top level was accommodation, with a smaller penthouse level sat atop it. Below that was a level of bars and eateries. Third level down housed the casinos and other "places of entertainment" and the bottom level was staff and admin. The team split up into small groups. I let each go their own way then decided to find a bar.

The place was busy, a mix of civvies and off- duty forces. The main walkway was lined with a selection of garish-looking places, advertised by neon signs, most with loud, repetitive music pumping out of them. I spotted a group of tall figures ahead and ducked into a bar doorway as a group of Marines strode confidently by. My caution was justified. From their arm flashes I could see they were from the Hoyle 4 base whose CO we'd embarrassed. Probably best they didn't see me here on my own, then.

Turning round, I could see I'd stumbled into one of the few quiet bars. It had a low light, moody ambience and a jazz quartet played softly in the corner.

I was happily on my fourth scotch and wowing the waitress with my dazzling repartee, when Kaur beeped on my E-pad.

"Sorry, Skip. There's been some trouble. Meet me at the Police HQ, Unit B cells on Level Four."

A guy couldn't even get quietly pissed in peace, it seemed. I downloaded and consulted the station guide and found my way to the cop shop. Once there, I flashed my ID at the guy on the desk and he summoned a cop who took me through to where Kaur was waiting outside the cells. She motioned through the spy-hole, I peered in to see Haugen sat inside, head in hands.

"What happened?" I asked.

The cop who walked me through cleared his throat and began reading from his E-pad.

"At 19.35 I was summoned to The Blue Lagoon Bar, where I witnessed the prisoner in violent altercation with a group of other customers. I, and three other officers ,attempted to -"

"Can we cut to the chase?" I snapped. "Let me speak to him."

The cop looked most put out and began a ramble about procedure and regulations. I'm not normally one for pulling rank but was losing my appetite for officialdom and its rules. So I read him the riot act, waved my chip implant at his machine, which immediately flagged up my security level, and told him I'd have him posted to Bumfuck, Outer Outer Rim if he didn't get that door open, pronto.

That did the trick and I entered the cell, the big man not even looking up at me. I sat next to him and offered a syg. The cop started to say "No smoking allowed" before wisely shutting his trap.   Haugen was in bits and, between sobs, told me about how he'd helped carry out several of the hostages, including a number of children, many of whom later died. I put my arm as far as I could around the huge shoulders and said "Come on,let's get you back to our digs."

I stood him up and we walked out, with not a peep from the cop. I beeped Wiz on the way back and asked him to meet us at the apartments so he could sit down and have a proper one to one with Haugen.

I cursed myself for not picking up on this earlier; a

good leader should be aware of his team's moods. I guess I'd been too wrapped up in my own anger. I made a mental note to schedule some time with Wiz for each of the team. That situation dealt with, I gave up on trying to get drunk and instead hit the sack for some shuteye.

Fourteen hours later I was woken by a hammering on the apartment door. Groggy and blurry-eyed, I dragged myself out of my pit and, wrapping a sheet around myself, answered. It was the cops.

"I thought we'd sorted this out," I grumbled. "Haugen was just drunk and upset."

The lead cop flashed a shark-like grin. "This isn't about Haugen, Mr Naylor. It's your man Schrader. He's under arrest for murder."

So, after a quick shower and a mug of tea, I found myself back at Police HQ. The cop who'd brought me in showed me to an office, where I sat around for ten minute kicking my heels. Then in came a guy in a rumpled suit, introducing himself as Simic, officer in charge of the case.

He offered me a syg then gave me the sitrep. Seems Schrader had started an argument at a gaming table in the main casino. The words led to fists which then led to someone being stabbed to death in a "frenzied attack". Schrader had been holding the knife when arrested and was covered in the victim's blood. Simic painted it as cut and dried. Then he made his pitch.

"Look, I know you military types are under a lot of pressure. A man can snap, right? Problem is, what your boy did here... well that usually draws a fifteen year sentence, minimum, and that's with a lenient judge. Fifteen years on a penal colony..."

I sighed inwardly and waited for it. Sure enough, a short pause and then it came. Simic gave me his best friendly smile and a conspiratorial wink.

"Lucky for you, I have some influence in this place. You know, for the right consideration, I'm confident we can smooth this whole thing over. An easy transfer, you and your boy could be on your way within 24 hours."

Pitch made, he smiled again and leant back in his chair. I returned his smile, then stood sharply and moved towards him, hand extended. He rose and met my handshake, smile turning to grimace as I squeezed hard and twisted on his fingers. I pulled him towards me and whispered in his ear.

"Listen, you prick, I'm not falling for your bullshit. I don't know what occurred to land my man in here but I do know this. You won't get a single credit out of us, you dirty filth. Now, I want to see Schrader and right away, or I'll break your fucking wrist, clear?"

Simic hissed and pulled his hand from mine. The

smile was gone, replaced by a look of pure venom.

"Okay, soldier boy. If that's how you want it but you've been out in space too long. You don't understand how things work round here. You can see your boy right now. You can be the one who tells him he'll be rotting in a prison mine for the rest of his days, too."

He stormed out of the room, calling for one of the other cops. I exhaled and rolled out the tension in my shoulders, hoping I'd made the right call. Shit, I was sure I had. Once you started dealing with lowlifes like this, they had their hooks in you. Plus, if it got out that a unit like AT5 was prepared to deal with Cartel, because that's no doubt who Silic worked for, then any reputation we had would be shot. A few minutes later, I was sat in a cell with a pale and shaken Schrader.

His side of the story was a little different, but not much.

"They were fleecing me, Skip," he told me. "I should've seen it coming but, to be honest, I just wanted to gamble without thought. I was hundreds down before I twigged the dealer was in on it. I confronted him, he denied it. But then I told the little fucker exactly how he was doing it. I've done a bit of card sharping in my time, you can't kid a kidder. That's when things got nasty. Ended up with him pulling a knife on me. We struggled. Well, I guess Vitali's training kicked in. Before I knew it, the knife was turned back on him and he'd been stabbed in the chest. One stab, that was it, he dropped. Lucky shot, I guess you could call it." He looked around at the cell walls. "Or maybe not."

I told him to hang on in there and not to worry, I would sort it. Inside, I wasn't so confident. Dealing with Army personnel was one thing, police and security were another; especially in these minor systems where the Cartel had growing influence. On leaving Schrader, I called up the team for a meet back at the apartments. Some of them were there already, the rest filtering in. I noticed a few black eyes and split lips and raised an eyebrow.

"Marines," chuckled Chen. "From Hoyle 4. Don't worry, you should see them."

I explained the situation and opened the floor. Kuruk suggested getting Carswell and CIHQ involved. I wasn't so sure, it would take time and I didn't want us hanging around here. Likewise, there was no way I was leaving our flyboy here on his own. Javez put forward the idea of hacking the police mainframe and soon lost me in a maze of tec talk. I stopped her mid-flow

"Okay, listen. You boffins put your heads together and let me know what can and can't be done. In the meantime, I'll whistle up some scran."

As we spoke, the story was getting reported on the

local media and Kuruk let me know we had another problem.

"It's the victim, Skip, one Stefan Erskine. Turns out his brother is an upper tier Cartel boss. Judging from the available intel, I'd say that big brother got little brother the job at the Casino. As you guessed, the place is pretty much Cartel run."

"Shit." I moved into the main room. Dutton was napping on the sofa. I nudged him awake. "Dutton, do me a favour, take Armstrong and head down to the cop shop. I want you to stand watch over Schrader, turns out his vic has Cartel connections."

Dutton yawned and stretched. "I'm on it, Skip."

That sorted, I went into the back room to check with the intel team. They were putting the finishing touches to a plan. I asked Mir to explain it to me in words of one syllable.

Basically, he explained, they could hack the police mainframe, get access to the CCTV and door locks. In theory, we could walk in and walk out with our man. Of course, we'd have to leave the station straight away and could never return. There was also the question of an arrest warrant going out, but no one would take much notice of that once we were out of the system. A bigger concern was any Cartel comeback; that was something we'd just have to deal with as and when.

Decision made, we put the plan into operation. The whole team moved out back to *Lady Luck* in dock, Mir and Javez were able to work their magic from there. Everyone else was on stand-by, in case we needed back-up. I had Kaur ready the ship for immediate take-off. Once all that was sorted, I took Vitali, Pops and McNulty with me. We went in on the graveyard shift, 0300 hours. The Station ran a 24/7 set up but, even so, I figured fewer staff would be on duty that time of morning.

I was right. There was one bod on the desk and he jumped to attention when I flashed the DIS ID that Slade had knocked up for me earlier. As we went in, the lights flickered for a second. I took that as a sign that Mir was working his magic. Sure enough, when the desk cop checked his terminal, the prisoner transfer was in the system and had been confirmed.

Dutton and Armstrong were still in position outside the cell area, it seemed the locals had no objection to them being there. Within minutes, Schrader was cuffed up and we bundled him out of the place sharpish, making a big show of shouting at the prisoner and giving him the occasional slap. The guy on the desk barely looked up as we exited. That's the good thing with REMFS, as long as the computer says yes, they don't ask questions.

Thirty minutes later we were nosing out of the dock and heading into the depths of the system. Kaur had sorted an RV with *Poseidon.* We met up with them in orbit at the fourth planet. Once on board, I asked to see the Captain in private and explained the situation to her. Being a good sort, she adjusted her log to remove any trace of us; if anyone checked the records we would have disappeared into space. Two jumps, then we were dropped off and were soon back home.

For the first time since leaving the *Utopis,* I turned my E-pad back on, to find several, increasingly irate messages from Carswell. Once I was settled back into the office I called him and took a carpeting. I don't think his heart was in it, though. He knew the set up, he knew we don't leave anyone behind. Still, he had a job to do and boxes to tick, like the rest of us. I also took the opportunity to register my own official and un-official thoughts on the nerve gas situation and the death of Jacobs.

The following day, back at base, we said goodbye to our comrade. There was a small plot of ground at the rear of the complex, overlooked by some trees. A nice, quiet spot. It was there we laid Jacobs to rest. Vitali said a few words. H was always good in these circumstances and we each said goodbye to Jacobs in our own way. I gave the team the rest of the day off to get their ground legs back, telling them that normal training and routines would resume the next day.

CHAPTER 13

CHARLIE FOXTROT 9

A couple of weeks later, I was putting some time in on the pistol range with Chen and Weaver when Carswell buzzed my E-pad to announce he was on base. I left the guys to it and headed to my office. Carswell was already there, helping himself to a shot of brandy from the bottle hidden in my drawer. As I parked my arse in the chair, he flicked a folder across the desk.

"First off, tell your people to watch their backs. The Erskine murder, nothing official has gone out but word is that the Cartel are onto it. Tell your boy to stay away from the tables for a while."

I nodded and picked up the folder.

"Will do, Chief. So, what's this?"

"New job, a big one."

I opened the folder and glanced down the first page.

"Copernicus 9. That's the clusterfuck place, right?"

"You could say that. What started off as a labour dispute has escalated into full scale war. The whole thing has been mis-managed. We've had ground forces in there for five months now, whatever we put in the Sparts match."

"So why not send in the Navy? Battlecruiser overhead, the usual business?"

"Because of what is there. Copernicus 9 is one of the few sources of deuteronium and also the largest. There are huge deposits there, we can't afford to damage the facilities or equipment."

"And deuteronium is a major component of the Murukami Drive."

"Exactly. And without the drives we are back to the old days of months of travel within a system, let alone the possibility of using SysGates."

"Why not drop a neutron bomb or maybe some kind of nerve agent?"

Carswell caught my scowl and had the grace to look almost shamefaced. But only for a second, then he continued.

"We thought about the bomb. Copernicus 9 has a somewhat unconventional magnetic field. We don't know if it's because of the deuteronium or other factors but the planet effectively screws up electronics. Coms work intermittently so there's no hope of using guided missiles. Even E-pads play up, from what I've been told. As for nerve agents, after the Lucerne debacle, no one would agree to that. Well, apart from a few hard-liners. Besides, gassing an entire population would be a major propaganda coup for the Sparts."

I shrugged and helped myself to a shot of my own brandy. "So, what's the op?"

"We have intel that three of the major Spart leaders will be on planet next month. One is already there, Trey Huxley. She is effective CinC on the ground. We believe that Louka Navarro and Fillion Joyner are en route to meet her there."

"Joyner, that name rings a bell. I think Devlin mentioned it, from his time at the ICA."

Carswell turned to a page in the folder and pointed. A mugshot of a tough looking guy in his mid-forties stared back at me. Carswell nodded.

"Joyner is the main go-between for the Sparts and the Cartel. He is chief negotiator when it comes to financial affairs according to our intel. So grabbing him would be a major fly in the ointment for the whole Spart operation, not just at Copernicus 9".

"Okay. If they are shipping in, why not blockade the planet and blast everything that appears in its atmosphere?"

"It's not that simple. There's the EMF problem I mentioned before. Sensors are affected a good distance away from the planet. As it is, SOP is to land troops in shuttles then transport them overland to the front line. The locals have good AA defences too."

Carswell helped himself to more of my booze.

"The Sparts are strong throughout the system. They can land on any of the other planets or moons and sneak in a small transport from there. Space is big, Naylor, even a battlecruiser can only cover so much."

I shrugged. "Okay, if we can't blockade the planet, why not just blockade the SysGate?"

"The Navy have a constant presence at the gate, there is only one in the system. But - and this is strictly between you and me - the Sparts have access to FTL ships."

"Faster than light? Fuck! So they can pop into the system anywhere, they don't need the gate?"

Carswell nodded. Another thought struck me.

"How come the Sparts have FTL when most of our own forces don't? We have to M- drive and SysGgate everywhere!"

"It's a new development, Naylor. I mentioned the Cartel before. Well, links between them and the Sparts are growing stronger. The Cartel are powerful and rich, getting richer. You've seen for yourself, places like

Utopis make them a lot of money."

"Can't we shut those places down?"

"It's tricky. There are local laws to consider, plus political will. Money buys politicians as well as guns. There's also the question of our resources."

"Our resources?"

"Yes, they are limited. War is not popular at the best of times, even less so when you are fighting your own citizens. As the rebellion spreads, the TA has less resources coming in. We are over-stretched, that's one reason for setting up units such as ours. A small squad is much more cost efficient to deploy than half the Space Fleet. Now you see why it is so important we prevent these links developing where we can."

I swore under my breath and jabbed the open folder with my finger. "So we go in and snatch them? In the middle of an urban battlefield? On a planet that screws up electronics?"

"That's about it. Oh, there is one other thing."

I raised my eyebrows as Carswell stood and headed for the door. He paused and turned in the doorway to deliver the punch line.

"The average temperature at the facility on Copernicus 9 this time of year is minus ten centigrade, daytime. You might want to pack a jumper. I've sent all the details to your E-pad, good luck!"

With that he was gone. I immediately paged Kaur and Kuruk to begin pre-planning then looked, with annoyance, at my empty brandy bottle.

An hour later the full team was assembled in the Briefing Room. I ran through the general background to the conflict then handed over to Kaur for more of the specifics. She had pinned a large map up onto the board.

"There's no satellite imagery available, but here are the original mining company survey maps. The mining operation is built into the side of this large chasm, a deep rift in the ground running north to south. It's a kilometre wide in places. The bulk of the operation is on the west side of the rift. Around that is the Complex, more on that later. We will be landing at the main transport base, known as the Hub. It's an air terminal about 120 klicks west of the Complex, linked by a single road."

"Why so far away?" asked Weaver. "Surely it increases costs to move material so far from the mine?"

Kaur nodded. "Agreed, but remember the EMF problem that Skipper mentioned? That distance is the nearest they could put an airfield to the mine without too much effect on the ATC systems. As it is, they still have problems and tend to rely on some rather old-style tec." She turned back to the map and indicated a blue line leading from the Hub.

"This is the road. It's a two lane highway, pretty much

a straight line. The local topography is flat, everything sits on this large plain." She indicated a spot halfway along the road. "This is a travel stop on the road, known as the Station. It has fuelling facilities, canteen, rest rooms and so on."

"How long does that drive take, then?" asked Javez.

"It's very dependent on the weather. The winters are harsh and heavy snowstorms sweep across the plains with little warning. When that happens, traffic slows to a crawl or even to a full stop. Once the storm has passed, they send snowploughs out to clear the way again."

"And this is the only route in to supply our forces?" Pops asked.

Kuruk stood up. "Yes, it is. At present, we have a main command and supply centre established at the Hub, along with facilities for the troops. There is a smaller post at the Station and the rest of our forces are based on the outskirts of the Complex. Before we get on to that, let's look at our targets."   Kuruk stepped to the front of the room, dimmed the lights and lowered the viewing screen.

"Full reports have been sent you each of your E-pads. However, here are the most recent footage and pictures we have of the trio in question."

Various clips of surveillance footage were displayed on the screen, along with some static pictures and news reports. Kuruk gave a brief commentary to each, then paused.

"And here is a special treat for you. A short clip of drone footage from the frontline."

The group gasped as a panoramic view unfolded on the screen. The drone floated slowly up to a height of around thirty metres and panned slowly from left to right. The picture was grainy and flickered with interference but we could see, in the immediate foreground, a white landscape scarred by trench lines. The lines led up to and ran along a low ridge, beyond which lay what can only be described as an urban inferno. It looked like a mouth to Hell, a mouth filled with broken, rotted teeth. Skeletal girders, empty windows, grey, smoked-stained concrete. Block upon block of devastated apartment buildings, rubble strewn streets and, here and there, the squat bulk of a factory or processing plant. Flames flickered in the ruins and over the whole lot hung a heavy pall of thick, black smoke.

"Bend over, here it comes again," was Weaver's response and not unwarranted, I thought. The footage ran for another few seconds before dissolving into static. Kuruk brought the lights back up as a low buzz of conversation filled the room.

"Alright, alright." I raised a hand for order.

"Questions?"

Saltzmann stood rather formally and asked, "How exactly are we supposed to find these three targets amidst such... such chaos?"

Kuruk took the floor again. "We have very good intel on their movements and expected whereabouts. We have a man on the inside."

McNulty lifted a hand. "How well can we trust this man of yours?"

"Oh he is extremely trustworthy." Kuruk gave a cadaverous grin. "You see, he is my brother."

Having delivered the good news, we spent the next few of hours poring over the maps and footage in detail. Kuruk pulled up detailed survey maps of the Complex itself. He pointed out the elevators and ore silos perched on the lip of the chasm. Adjacent was a band of processing plants, large grey blocks with masses of pipework that led waste away to recycling plants out at the ends of the Complex. In front of those lay an area comprising storage buildings, transport hubs and factories. This, in turn, was bordered by a service area, housing vehicle and maintenance depots, engineering workshops and the like. On the outer edge of the Complex, furthest away from the Rift, were the worker accommodation blocks, leisure facilities and various support buildings.

Kuruk pointed out each area in turn, highlighting key buildings and likely command posts for the Spart leaders. He then showed us the far side of the Rift. There were only a few buildings there, on account of the ground sloping steeply up into a range of hills. Not good for building on, however they did give good cover to Spart forces, who could be fed piecemeal through narrow passes, then filtered across the narrow Rift bridges and into the Complex. Kuruk turned from the screen to face the group again.

"All in all the Complex is just under twelve klicks long and five klicks across at its widest point. In theory you could drive from the outer edge to the Rift in about twenty minutes. Not any more, though. The first Commander on the ground had the genius notion of bombarding the Sparts into surrender. He set up base at the Hub, then established a frontline just outside the Complex. He had five units of ground artillery shipped in and they pounded the place for three days. Granted, they were careful not to hit any of the important facilities further in but he failed to appreciate two facts. First, given the importance of the Complex, the major buildings were built and designed to withstand major shocks, be they man made or natural. Second, those buildings that were affected by the bombardment became rubble strewn fortresses, an ideal setting for defenders working against stronger forces. The first wave of armour and infantry that were sent in never came back."

Kuruk keyed his E-pad and more footage ran on the screen. Helm-cam footage from some poor grunt, no doubt. He continued.

"The first Commander's replacement thought he could crack the Complex by applying even more force. He sent in several waves of ground attack units, most of which were swallowed up in the flames and rubble. Our troops have technically better equipment but the advantage is lost in the smoke filled ruins, where fighting is often face to face. Add to that the problem with electronics and suddenly old school tec looks decidedly the better option."

As if to verify the point the footage, which by now was showing the wearer under heavy small arms fire, flickered before disappearing altogether. Kuruk hit the pause button.

"Weeks of fighting with no gains and increasing casualty lists saw the second Commander heading home, too. The third Commander was rather more cautious. He established dug-in positions on the plain in front of the Complex and decided on a war of attrition. There is little in the way of natural resources on the planet, all supplies are shipped in. The Navy set up as much of a blockade above as they could, then everyone waited. Of course, there were a few things that no one had counted on. First was the weather. A month in, temperatures began to drop and snow began to fall. Bad enough if you are in a ruined complex but even worse out on the exposed plain."

"How the frick can anyone be surprised by the weather?" interjected Wiz. "That's surely a basic part of planning?"

Kuruk grimaced. "You would think so, wouldn't you? It seems, however, that the powers that be in this case anticipated that the Sparts would roll over at the first sign of our ground troops. They planned on a quick operation, days, maybe a week or two at the most. As the situation developed, it seems no one at Supreme Command thought to plan ahead. No one there knew that the weather on Copernicus 9 would change so quickly, no one had the foresight to check."

"I'm starting to see why this place got the name Clusterfuck 9," muttered Chen.

"Quite." Kuruk nodded. "The second surprise was the resourcefulness of the Sparts in shipping in supplies. With Cartel help, they are well supplied with food, weapons and ammo."

"Things come in threes," said Pops. "What was the

third surprise?"

Kuruk gave a tight smile. "The third surprise was the counterattack. During the first major storm of the season, a Spart attack force came screaming out of the blizzard to hit the Hub. Not a large force and many of them were killed in the attack, but supplies were raided, ammo dumps destroyed, personnel killed or captured. The raiders hit hard, then faded back into the blizzard."

Kuruk taaped on his E-pad again to bring a mugshot up on the screen. A silver-haired Army Colonel in his 60s stared determinedly out at us.

"This is the fourth and current Commander, Colonel Behr. He's been in charge for eight weeks and is the man we are to liaise with on arrival. He has strengthened positions on the plain and established perimeter patrols. Rather than push headlong assaults into the rubble, he is working to contain the Sparts and gradually shrink their perimeter piecemeal. Our forces are concentrated into assaults on specific areas, attempting to take the Complex building by building. A slow process, of course, made all the more difficult by the weather and unusual conditions."

I called for a ten minute coffee break, then reconvened for an open session. Unlike conventional Army briefings, we open the floor to all present. After all, each unit member's an expert in their field. Given the nature of our task, we decided to form three main front line teams; one for each of the targets, plus a Command Group incorporating Coms and Intel. Another team would stay upstairs with the Navy to act as liaison and reserve. I took a few minutes to gather my thoughts before assigning roles.

"Team Red, Koenig, Armstrong, Williams." The three nodded and moved to stand together.

"Team Blue, Khan, McNulty, Dutton. Team White, Vitali, Weaver, Haugen." Each also nodded in turn and moved into their groups.

"Team Green, reserve. Mir, Slade, Kaur." I looked over at Buresi. "Doc, I'd like you as Medic, with Kuruk and Slade on Intel. Javez, you're on Coms. Devlin, I want you as a roving sniper for back up. Pops and I are the Command. Schrader, you'll be taking us in as close as you can. Once we are on the ground I want you to oversee transport and logistics."

Schrader smiled. "No problem, Skip."

"Alright. Those of you not assigned get to stay here and keep warm. But I want you ready to move at short notice, in case we need back up. The rest of you, assemble at the main hangar in ninety minutes. Bring whatever personal gear you want, we'll pick up whatever else we need en route. Kuruk, can you find out what the locals are equipped with and get us the same?

I want us to blend in, not show up with the latest, clean gear. "

Kuruk made a note on his E-pad.

"We can go over deployment and other details on the way. Pops, Armstrong, let's visit the armoury and see what we can rustle up. Okay people, move, move, move!"

The fortunates hurried out of the room, the wheelchair-bound Bahadur blowing a kiss and calling out "Hurry back, I miss you already!"

CHAPTER 14

WELCOME TO HELL

Schrader carefully guided *Lady Luck* through the stratosphere and pulled level just above the layer of heavy cloud. He was flying on manual, most of the instrument dials were spinning madly. Schrader ignored them all, bringing the transport down by feel as much as anything else. He had been in contact with ATC at the Hub, we were now bearing down on them. A pulse beacon had been set up below and enough of a signal broke through the interference for our flyboy to get a decent fix. We descended into white, swirling snow, the transport bucking in the fierce winds. Nothing was visible through the front screen except a blanket of grey dotted with heavy flakes.

At fifty metres there was a break in the gloom and below we could make out a flashing light. Schrader lined up on it and took us in. Sometimes you just can't beat the

Mark One Eyeball. The coms hissed static but our earlier transmission from upstairs had been obviously been received as, if by magic, two parallel rows of lights appeared on the ground. Schrader took us in for a perfect landing on the wind-swept runway. Vitali, as was his custom, crossed himself on landing. Buttoning up our snow jackets, we stood and prepared to disembark.

White clad figures approached as the rear ramp lowered, allowing the biting wind into the interior. Within minutes, with assistance from the ground crew, we were unloaded and assembled in an only slightly warmer hangar. Well, at least the wind wasn't cutting through us in here though it made its presence felt by howling around the buildings. A figure in a hooded Army parka strode over, the silver haired Colonel who's picture we'd seen before. I snapped off a salute, which he returned, then shook my hand warmly.

"Behr. You must be Naylor? CIHQ told me you were coming, welcome to our icy home."

"Thank you, sir. I trust you've been apprised of our requirements?"

"Indeed. If you'd like to follow Munroe here, we've sectioned off a private space for you. I'll have catering get some hot food over, that way you won't be seen by other personnel. I gather I am to keep your presence here quiet?"

"Thank you, sir, that's most helpful. Hopefully we can get our job done and be out of your hair before you know it. Perhaps we could meet in an hour and I can run you through our Ops outline?"

"Indeed. I'll instruct Munroe to stay on hand. He'll bring you over to my office when you are ready."

We exchanged salutes again and Behr moved off. We followed the white clad figure of Munroe and were soon ensconced in a reasonably comfortable cold weather shelter, shovelling away hot stew. That done, I had a quick a meeting with Behr, then a final briefing and equipment check with the team. After that, we got our heads down for the night, planning on moving up to the front line before dawn. Where possible we wanted to keep our arrival quiet and unnoticed.

My E-pad beeped at still-dark-o-clock. Shivering, I dressed quickly and went out into the main room. The team were assembling, grunting and coughing as they did so. Schrader came in through the external door, followed by an icy draught. He'd been up and about organising our transport. We filed out to two white-painted APCs, engines humming as they waited in the snow. I had the heavy gear loaded into one of them. The snow had stopped and there was a faint, pre-dawn light so, while the loading was going on, I took the opportunity to have a look round the place.

The Hub was little more than a group of hangars and staff quarters, expanded by prefab military buildings and ammo and supply dumps. A wire fence ran around the perimeter with only one gateway in and out, manned by a checkpoint crew. Beyond it lay the single road leading off to the Complex. On each side, flat plains, dusted with snow, stretched off into the foggy distance. There wasn't a tree or shrub in sight. Not a place you wanted to be caught out in the open, I thought.

Keeping sidearms and personal kit about ourselves, we squeezed into the other vehicle. Our driver turned, gave a cheery grin and shouted "All aboard for the ride, once round the harbour!"

Over-shoulder bars held us in place but it was a shaky ride nonetheless and I was glad, at this point, we hadn't stopped for breakfast. After a couple of hours, the APCs came to a halt and the rear door hummed open. We shuffled out into an enclosed area surrounded by a three meter high concrete barrier. A light snow had begun to fall and the morning was overcast and grey. I felt colder already. A soldier in grubby, winter combat gear jogged over to us and threw up a salute.

"Sergeant Abadi, I'm your liaison officer. The Colonel said I'm to show you to your quarters. We've allocated a platoon bunker for you at the end of the line that is no longer - er - required, so if you could follow me please, sir."

"Thank you, Sergeant." I returned his salute. "Lead on."

Schrader was overseeing the loading of our bulkier equipment onto sleds. The rest of us lined up after Abadi and followed him in single file, going through a gap in the barrier and into a gloomy trench network, at the start of which someone had stuck a crude sign saying *Welcome to Hell*. The Sergeant paused and turned.

"If I could advise, please keep your heads down below the parapet at all times. Don't be tempted to take a peek, their snipers love sightseers."

I nodded and passed the message down the line. We soon arrived at a dug-in bunker system situated at the south end of the trench network, set back a short distance from the front line. The Sergeant showed us in, told us how to contact him if we needed anything, then left us to settle into our new home.

The main dug-out comprised of a central chamber, the main feature of which was a solid fuel stove that was piping out some very welcome heat. There were gear lockers against one wall, two tables in the centre and some racking and a large whiteboard on the far wall. A curtained doorway led to a small galley and ablutions facilities. Two other openings led to corridors, off which were bunk rooms. We flicked on the lights, stowed gear and I got a brew on while Kuruk and Slade began laying out maps and pinning up charts. Given the problems with electronics, we had decided to keep things old school and work with paper and pens. Once everyone was settled and had a mug of tea in their hands, Slade called us over, indicating the large charts he had fixed to the wall.

"These plans are from the architect that designed the Complex. They show the various subterranean systems that run under the whole area. Sewers, maintenance tunnels, access points to the main mines and ventilation shafts. These will be our points of access."

Weaver raised a hand. "If we know about these tunnels I'm guessing the Sparts do too?"

Slade nodded. "They probably do but perhaps not all of them. You see here, here and here?" He pointed to one of the charts. "These are construction tunnels, used purely during the building of the complex. They are not as extensive as the main networks but do provide access to them in certain places. We are hopeful that these tunnels are not known to the locals. They appear only on these construction charts."

As Slade briefed us, Armstrong and McNulty were checking the weapons. They had already stripped and cleaned everything en route, but they liked to be sure. Given the conditions, we had also gone old school for our firearms. A stash of SMGs, a couple of trusty AK's, basic pistols and frag grenades. While they had no circuits to go wrong, they did require maintenance, especially in these conditions. Slade continued.

"We have marked ground level entry points in red. As you can see, each lies within the perimeter so we will need to go into the Complex in order to access the tunnels. For that reason, we have decided to operate at night. Kuruk?"

Kuruk put down his mug of tea and moved over to the charts.

"We are hoping the Sparts will be less vigilant after dark. The Colonel has informed us that there is little activity at night, partly due to the temperature of course. It can go down to minus thirty. Everyone will be equipped with NVGs. We are hoping they will operate okay under the conditions here, if not I'm afraid we will be relying on torches. We will settle in today, then tonight each team will carry out a recce. I've marked each relevant access point."

Khan raised a hand. "How do we get across the open ground and into the Complex?"

Slade smiled. "Leg power, I'm afraid. Any engine noise will be picked up, so we go in slow and silent. As you can see, we have marked out a route for each team. We will also arrange help, where we can, from any of our forces within the Complex. What we don't know is what the conditions are like down there. The tunnels could be blocked with rubble, for example, or they may have been barricaded or fortified. So the recce is purely to take a looksee and to place some surveillance equipment. Javez?"

Javez brought forward a kit bag, unzipping it and taking out a circular, dull metallic device.

"Each team will have five of these devices to deploy. They will transmit audio and visual back to us, we hope. There is no guarantee they will work properly under the conditions but, if they do, we can at least keep eyes on the tunnels." She looked over to me and I stood to address the group.

"Everyone clear? We get in, get out, nothing more."

I rolled up my sleeve. We had all been issued with old fashioned watches, the battery type with moving hands.

"Synchronise watches please. I have 0717. Sunset is 1720. The teams will move out at 1930. Devlin will be taking up position prior to that in order to give any covering fire. We have some time, I suggest Javez brief us all on how to deploy the devices, we get a comsnet set up, then we all get some rest before heading out."

As the group gathered round Javez, I nudged Pops and asked him to join me outside. We buttoned up against the cold and stepped back out into the main trench system. After a few minutes we found Abadi's post and, knocking on the entrance, went in. He was sat next to a corporal who was twisting the dial on an old fashioned radio set.

"My word, a battle tranny," Pops grinned. "I've not seen one of those for a while."

Abadi looked up. "I know." He turned back to the operator. "Carry on, Sharman, give me a shout if you get anything." He turned back to us.

"We're trying to raise one of our forward command posts. We find this old gear works better than the new stuff. Trouble is, it's temperamental first thing in the morning. Bit like my first wife."

I smiled. "I was wondering if we could get a look at the place. Would also appreciate advice on approach routes into the Complex, we're sending teams in at night."

Abadi raised his eyebrows. "Night ops? Good luck with that! Okay, follow me, sir."

The three of us wound our way through the trench system, Abadi nodding to various soldiers here and there. Our breath hung smoke-like in the lightening air. Within minutes I couldn't feel my cheeks. Pops chuckled at my discomfort, the old bastard was as tough as they come. As we got nearer to the front line, I noticed that most of the troops had a hollow-eyed look about them. I questioned Abadi about it.

"Most of them have been here for the duration. They switched Commanders but the higher ups seems to have forgotten the Poor Bloody Infantry."

"Shit," I replied. "Months, in this?"

Abadi smiled sadly. "We have it easier here than the teams in the rubble. Though we've usually had an artillery strike by this time of day. The rising sun lights up our positions beautifully and our friends have had plenty of time to get our range."

The trench narrowed and we moved in single file. Abadi continued. "The trench system was supposed to act as containment and also as a rest area for our troops. Units are rotated into the Complex on a regular basis. We have to maintain a presence there in order to keep hold of any gains we've made. Otherwise, we clear a building, we move out, the Sparts move right back in and we are back to square one. Almost half our troops are out there, fighting day and night. We call them Rubble Rats. Take a look."

We had reached a circular emplacement at the end of the line. Abadi nodded to the soldier occupying it, who moved aside to allow me to look into his binoscope. I moved back my hood and pressed my face to the rubber eyepiece. I couldn't help but swear under my breath. Seeing drone footage was one thing, seeing the Complex for real was a visceral experience.

Across a blasted plain it lay, a lunar landscape, sprinkled with snow. The rays of the morning sun lent the whole scene a deceptive, rosy glow and made squat shadows out of the buildings. Here and there, the sun sparkled off a piece of glass or metal, though there was little left in the way of complete windows.

There was total silence and stillness, no bird song, last night's wind had died away. It almost looked like a painting, some artist's interpretation of a post-Apocalyptic landscape. Twisted girders, rubble, the looming bulk of grey buildings... and even at this range an odour that stung the nostrils, a smell of burning wood, burning flesh and brick dust. My musings were interrupted by the soldier shouting, "Incoming!"

We threw ourselves down into the freezing slush as the whistle of shells screamed overhead. Within seconds we were embroiled in an inferno of noise, hissing shrapnel and eye-stinging smoke. It was the longest ten minutes of my life. At last the bombardment ceased and, ears ringing, I staggered to my feet. Even Pops looked a bit pale. From nearby trenches we could hear the calls for medics. Abadi brushed himself down, took out a syg packet and offered it around. He lifted the syg to his lips with a shaky hand and nodded to us.

"They must know you're here. That was by way of welcoming you, I reckon."

Pops took a long pull on his syg. "If it's all the same, I'd rather they just ignored us."

I took the proffered syg. "Once we've settled in, I'd like to get out into the Rubble, if it's do-able?"

Abadi nodded. "There's a rotation at 1130, one team in, one team out. If you can be at my post at 1120, I'll hook you up with them."

That sorted, it was time to get back in the warm and have some breakfast.

CHAPTER 15

INTO THE RUBBLE

A few hours later and I was back with Abadi, solo this time. I didn't want to draw any more attention to the rest of the team than was necessary. He took me to another emplacement at the edge of the trench line where a group of around a dozen figures were gathered. Like Abadi, they were all dressed in grubby winter camo and I was glad I'd made the decision to equip the team with the same. All wore a blue armband on their right arm and Abadi handed me one over.

"We change these every couple of days." he explained. "It can get confusing out there."

Then he gestured to one of the group.

"That's Corporal Fisher, team leader. This lot are going in for a three day stint. When you want to come back they'll send you out with a guide."

I nodded, noticing that neither Fisher, or anyone else, was wearing rank insignia. Abadi continued with a grin. "I've told them you're on a fact finding mission for the higher ups, so I'm afraid they'll have marked you as a REMF."

I returned the grin. "No problem. The less they know for now, the better."

Abadi walked me over to the group. "Fisher, here's that obs guy I told you about."

Fisher, as gaunt-faced as the other troops I had seen, barely acknowledged my existence, muttering quietly, "Stick close, keep your head down, make no noise."

I nodded in reply and, as the group moved out, took up position as Arse-end Arnold. To our left, a gimpy began chattering, a lazy curve of tracer arcing out towards one of the large buildings on the edge of the Complex. To keep any sniper heads down, I guessed. One by one the team rolled over the edge of the trench to run at a low crouch to the nearest burnt out building.

Despite running and the winter suit, my toes were already numb. The cloud had cleared and the low sun was bright but gave off no heat. The team moved through the building, making barely any sound. At the exit on the other side, Fisher paused in the open doorway and gave a whistle. From the rubble and wreckage beyond, figures rose as if out of the ground. Within seconds, they were in the building with us. Their leader brushed snow and mud off his suit and took the syg offered by Fisher.

"Alright, Tom?"

Fisher nodded. "Karl. Yep, all fine. Only ten?"

The other man grimaced. "Yep. Sniper got Petrov yesterday morning and old Vaughnie disappeared last night."

"Shit. Anything else?"

Karl hawked and spat on the dusty floor. "FAU. The Sparts are still holding the Redhouse. We have a team on the ground floor but they are finding it tough going. They could probably do with some help."

"OK, we'll head there first. See you in a few days." Tom slapped the other man on the arm and turned back to the open doorway. While the two had been speaking, the outgoing team were handing over gear to their replacements. As well as weapons and grenades, I noticed crowbars and sledgehammers changing hands, too. At some unspoken signal, they then melted away back towards our lines and Fisher's group moved further into the Complex.

The smell here was worse. Far worse. The smell of death, of burning, of rubble and destruction. It clung to your clothes, it clung to your skin, your hair. I never could wash that smell away. For a long time after I would wake with it in my nostrils. Keeping my head down, I followed the back of the soldier in front. Within seconds I was lost, the place was a confused mess of ruins and debris-choked streets. Sometimes we moved through buildings, other times we crawled through the snow and mud. We climbed through broken windows and duck walked through large pipes. No one spoke; everyone was alert and vigilant, weapons were held ready, safeties off.

After about fifteen minutes we assembled in another ruin. Fisher glanced carefully through the window at the large redbrick building opposite. He called up two of the team and indicated the large opening on the first floor.

"In ten seconds, covering fire on that window. Then hold here and wait for my signal. The rest of you, with me. You…" this was directed to me. "Move fast, try not to get shot."

Two of the squad moved to the window and trained their SMGs upward. Fisher and the rest of us gathered near the door. Fisher shouted and kicked the door open and the two opened up with a stream of bullets. As one, the rest of us sprinted across the open ground towards the door in the large building opposite. It opened and a figure waved us in. A shot whistled over my head as I covered the last couple of metres, then I was inside and the door clanged shut behind me.

Fisher was already in conflab with the soldier who had waved us in. She was explaining the current sitrep.

I noticed that holes had been smashed in the walls so the whole downstairs of the building was open to view. It looked like some kind of warehouse or storage facility, though little remained of any shelving or other furniture.

Scattered around the place were maybe twenty troops. Some stood guard at the stairwell, others watched through the windows. Some just sat staring into space. One groaned in the corner, head swathed in a bloody bandage. Suddenly, there was a rattle of fire from upstairs and the crump of a grenade. Those sitting immediately sprang to life, moving to the stairwell and readying weapons. There was a shout from above.

"Travers here, coming in, two of us!"

Two figures hurtled down the stairs and began speaking in urgent tones to the female soldier, the senior officer, I guessed. She barked out commands and the group immediately began forming up into defensive positions. I was totally ignored, so I just readied my AK and took up a position in a corner. There was a rattle as a round object clattered down the stairs, then a bang and a blinding light. luckily, I'd averted my eyes but not everyone had been so quick. Rubbing eyes, many of them turned away from the flash. I trained my gun on the stairwell but the Sparts were cleverer than that.

With a series of dull thuds and a crash, a section of the ceiling came down above us, right in the centre of the room. Choking dust filled the air. Half a dozen faces appeared around the edge of the hole, followed by the rattle of small arms fire and the whine of bullets hitting concrete. I instantly dropped and rolled, sweeping my AK up to return fire. Others did the same, though I saw a number fall as they were hit. The female officer swore loudly and shouted.

"Galvez! Light 'em up! Covering fire!"

A number of the squad began concentrating their fire as a figure ran into the space under the hole, carrying a bulky tank on his back. With a manic laugh he pointed a nozzle upwards towards the hole. There was a hiss and a whoosh, the whole room was filled with searing heat as a jet of flame spurted up towards the Sparts.

Fisher shouted, "Grenades!" and those of his squad still standing immediately unpinned and hurled frag grenades up through the hole. Galvez ceased firing and moved back as the room above was filled with whirling fragments of steel.

Meanwhile, the female officer was shouting "Grab the wounded. Evac! Over the road!". A nearby figure was on the floor clutching a bloody leg. I grabbed his shoulder straps and dragged him out through the door we had come in by. The two squad members still in the building opposite opened up with their covering fire again and, in a matter of minutes, everyone was back in the smaller building. The officer huddled with a radio operator who was calling "Charlie Four, this is Alpha Two. We are moving back towards you now. We have wounded."

Fisher nudged the officer and indicated me. She came over, wiping back a strand of black hair from her face that had sneaked out from under her cap.

"Lieutenant Yao. I gather you are on an obs mission?" I nodded in reply.

"Thanks for pulling my man out," she said. "You looked handy with that AK, too."

I shrugged. "Beginner's luck, ma'am."

Yao gave me a wry grin. "OK, whatever you say. In any case, Mr Obs, we are evaccing this position. We've been trying to take the Redhouse for days but the Sparts have reinforced way beyond what we can keep up with. We are moving further over, to our main position in the Complex. You can come along but it will be more difficult for you to extract later. It's up to you."

I glanced at my watch. Shit, I had been here for barely an hour, it felt much longer than that. I thought of the team and the fact we were out on recce that night.

"I think I've seen enough for now ma'am. I'll head back out if you can spare a guide."

"No problem, Mr... I don't believe I caught your

name?"

Now it was my turn to smile. "I don't believe I gave it, Lieutenant. But thanks for your help, it's been most educational."

She returned the smile then looked away to assign me a guide, once more the professional soldier. Within minutes, I was on my way back to the relative comfort of the bunker.

In my absence the team had settled in and were mostly getting some shuteye. It's a rare soldier who doesn't take every opportunity to grab sleep where they can. I moved into the bunker quietly, got some scran sorted, then put my head down for a few hours.

I pulled myself by my elbows into the cover of a snow-filled ditch, lowered the NVGs to my eyes and scanned the rubble immediately ahead. The image was flickering but the interference was not too bad. Everything looked quiet. The three teams had worked their way into the complex earlier. Devlin had gone out a couple of hours prior to that to conduct a sweep of the area and set up a support fire position. It looked like it wouldn't be required but better to have him on the board. I nudged Javez, who lay next to me, gloved hands working the small coms unit. She looked up and shook her head. So far the coms had given us nothing but static. If any team ran into trouble the first we would know would be the distant sounds of gunfire. Presuming they weren't attacked while in the tunnels, of course.

Freezing though it was, I felt more useful out here in the field than waiting back in the bunker. Having said that, although the winter camo suits were good, you didn't want to expose yourself to this weather for any longer than necessary. Devlin had the worst job. A sniper may have to stay still for hours at a time, that took some discipline in these conditions. Javez nudged me. She brought her face close to mine and I pulled back my hood so she could whisper in my ear.

"Team Blue report job done, they are on the way back. It was a weak signal but it came through. Still nothing from the others."

I nodded and replaced my hood. I gave her a thumbs up and signalled that we should return to base. A short while later, we were glugging hot drinks and warming ourselves by the stove. Not long after that, Team Blue came in, their access point was the closest to the bunker. Within an hour, both the other teams had returned and we gathered for a de-brief.

Blue had the best news. The path to the access point was relatively clear and the tunnel itself appeared unused and undiscovered. They had penetrated in as far as the first junction hatchway to the main service tunnel.

The hatchway looked unused, so they risked a peek through, into the wider, empty passageway beyond. They deployed their surveillance devices on each side of the hatch and returned.

Team Red had a reasonably clear run to the access point but found the tunnel blocked with rubble. Koenig had a probing device which indicated the rubble was only a metre or so deep but it would take some shifting, a noisy job in the dead of night.

Team White had the bad news. They hadn't been able to reach their access point. It was up at the north end of the Complex, not far from where I had been that morning. This was the most hotly contested area, dominated by a huge factory which had withstood numerous assaults from our forces. The zone was also under the eyes of Spart snipers who covered the area 24/7.

Vitali described the situation and made a suggestion, to which I agreed. As Team White had the furthest to travel, it made more sense for them to bunk down up at the north end of the trench complex. I told Vitali I would sort it with Abadi in the morning and also assigned Devlin to him for anti-sniper duties. As we would be running night ops, I briefed everyone that they wouldn't be expected to be active during daylight hours. They were to rest up as much as possible. We would have a daily briefing here at the main bunker at 1600 each day and all our ops would be under cover of darkness. It was 0200 by then, so I told everyone to turn in.

The next two nights passed quietly enough. Team Blue moved into the main tunnel and got as far as the edge of the main Spart stronghold. They placed more surveillance devices then sat back to get an idea of routines and movements.

Over two nights of careful, quiet digging, Team Red managed to clear their access point and gain entry to the main construction tunnel where they also deployed surveillance equipment and retreated. Team White, now operating from a shared bunker up north, had the unenviable job of working as bait for Devlin. Under his direction, they managed to draw out two Spart snipers who Devlin promptly slotted. They reached the access point too late to venture in that night though. No one wanted to be moving through that sector come daybreak, so they fell back to their bunker.

It was the next day that a cheerful Sergeant Abadi came to bid me goodbye.

"We're finally being relieved," he announced as he shook my hand. "Well, half of us are at any rate. The first batch of new units came in last night, we are exchanging today. Thought I'd come and let you know. I don't know who your new liaison will be but I'll make sure he's fully briefed."

I thanked Abadi for his assistance. When things are working well change makes me nervous. With good reason, as it turned out.

Just prior to our evening brief, the new liaison showed his face, Sergeant Floyd. He was efficient enough, a little wet behind the ears and "itching to have a crack at the Sparts". But he did his job and gave us no problems. Which is more than can be said for his commanding officer...

CHAPTER 16

CAPTAIN GAGE

We had a tough time of it that night. Team Red remained on surveillance duties, we were getting a decent signal from their devices. Over the last 24 hours, we were building up a good picture of Spart activity around the area. Blue and White went out, at a later time than before. We figured enemy activity would be at its lowest in the small hours of the morning. Both teams got caught out, though. Blue running into a tunnel patrol and getting involved in a firefight;White getting pinned down by two or more snipers before even reaching the access point. It seemed they had also brought in an anti-sniper, so Devlin had his work cut out to cover the team and to survive himself. Still, they all made it back just before daybreak and retired, exhausted, to their bunker.

It wasn't until around noon that I heard about the problem. Floyd came in as I was napping on my bunk to tell me that my team had been sent out on patrol with the regular grunts. I shot up at once, zipped into my outdoor outfit and headed north. Floyd guided me to the Central Command Post and I burst in without knocking.

"Who's in charge here?" I demanded. Four or five faces looked up at me from the operations table. The wireless operator stopped his dial twiddling to stare at me.

"That would be me. Captain Gage. Who the hell are you?" A short figure pushed his way towards me. I sized him up immediately. Immaculate uniform, including gongs, though none were for combat. A pockmarked face, the kind my old man used to say only a mother could love, sat atop a barrel chested body, I wondered if he had to get his uniforms tailored to fit. He was the type who wore his cap down low over his eyes and he sneered as he looked up at me. He seemed resolutely unimpressed by my shabby winter gear and stubbled face.

"I'm Naylor, Assault Team Five."

"Rank? You have no rank markings, man, what sort of outfit is this?"

I gritted my teeth. "CSM, sir, currently Acting Field

Commander of Special Unit Assault Team Five." I put emphasis on the *Special* in an effort to make my point. The effort was wasted.

"What do you mean by bursting in here like this? Look at the state of you, I should have you up on a charge! No wonder this operation is such a mess! No bloody discipline! Well, things are going to change round here!"

"Sir," I struggled to get a word in. "If I might, who are you and did you order my personnel out on patrol this morning?"

"I'm the new Commander for this sector. Arrived yesterday, in the nick of time it would seem. Shambles! And if your men are the lazy bunch sleeping in late then, yes I did send them out on patrol. You don't win battles by loafing around in your bunk!"

"Captain, those men are not part of your command, as I'm sure they would have told you. We are here on a special operation of our own."

"I've not been informed of that, Sergeant. All I know is that four men were still in their cots at reveille and three of them are now out on patrol!"

"Where is the fourth?"

"He refused my orders and was insolent! He is currently being detained pending charges and return to Rear Echelon."

I groaned and rubbed a dirty hand across my face. That

would be Devlin no doubt.

"Sir, if that is who I think it is, you are lucky he only insulted you rather than punched your lights out."

Gage bristled. "Well, I can see where your men get it from! Sergeant, I suggest that unless you want to be up on a charge, too- "

Now, you might be surprised to hear, given my occupation, that I'm not really a violent person. Maybe it was the strain of the operation. Maybe it was the thought of my people being put in unnecessary danger by a jumped-up REMF. Whichever, I decided on the direct approach.

I balled my fist into the front of Gage's tunic and lifted him up until his toes barely touched the floor. I pushed my face into his and growled low.

"Listen, you little turd. If any of my people gets so much as a scratch out there, I will slot you. If you ever try and order my people around again, I will slot you. If you so much as think about pressing charges on any member of my unit... I will slot you. In fact, right now you are going to have to work very hard to deter me from twisting your pointy little head around until it faces the other way. Clear?"

I dropped him then smoothed out the front of his tunic. His face was a picture, half shock at being spoken to in such a way, half pure fear. I could smell it on him.

The other faces at the table, all in clean, shiny uniforms, were aghast and pale with amazement. The radio operator, who had been here for a while judging by his look, was finding it hard to suppress his laughter. Red faced, he was pinching his lips together, shoulders heaving. Gage finally found his voice, turning to the operator.

"Get me Colonel Behr at once! You!" he turned back to me. "Get out of my sight before, before…" His threat went unheard as I turned my back on him and exited the bunker.

Outside in the trench I got a tip from a passing soldier as to where Devlin was being held. Ten minutes later, I had him out. Seething was not the word, I'd never seen him so agitated. I got him back to our HQ before he could do anything about it and sat him down with a drink. He explained what had happened. How, half asleep as they were, the team had been dragged out by Gage and his cronies and ordered out with the patrol. Technically, none of them had a foot to stand on, Gage was a superior officer and we were, after all, out in the field. I was surprised at Vitali's compliance, until Devlin pointed out that he had muttered it was easier to do the patrol than serve a life sentence for killing a Rodney.

By 1600 that evening the whole team was gathered back in our bunker. The patrol had largely been uneventful, the guys said, and Gage had been noticeable by his absence on their return. I'd heard no further news of charges, nor anything from Behr, so I presumed, for now, it was problem sorted and we could get back to the operation. As the team huddled round eating from their mess tins I ran over the plan.

"It's obvious the northern access point is proving too hot, so we will use Team White to reinforce Team Blue. You can stand down tonight, we will go back in tomorrow night. I want White and Blue to make plenty of noise once you are in the tunnels. I want the Sparts to think there may be a major force coming in through that route. Team Red, I'll be with you, we go in for another recon. One last check but if things are really quiet, then we go in and snatch whichever of the three Tangos we can. If not, we will repeat again the night after."

Heads nodded and Kuruk stood to address the group.

"Here's the latest word on the whereabouts of our targets. As you can see, two of them are in striking distance of Team Red. No word, though, as to the kind of security around them. Our source is also getting hints of some large operation being planned. Slade, you have more info?"

Slade placed down his mess tin.

"Yes. Coms with the Navy bods upstairs are limited

as you know, but they have reported an increase in Spart activity within the system. Faster Than Light leaves a trace at entry and exit points, it can be picked up for a few days after. Well, there has been a lot of FTL activity recently."

"Can't the Navy deal with them up there?" asked Armstrong. "Save us the bother of getting shot at?"

Slade, being Navy himself, bristled slightly. "It's not that easy. FTL ships can jump into any part of the system. We simply don't have the resources to cover the whole area. And even if we did, engaging a ship in space flight is not easy. The speeds alone make any missile or weapon fire largely inaccurate. If we can catch them in orbit or the outer atmosphere, there's a better chance. But then we have this damn eco-system playing havoc with our instruments!"

Kuruk interjected."You can see why the Sparts have chosen this place as their major battleground. Not only for the resources but the set up plays to their strengths. A victory here would be a major coup for them, it might nudge others who are currently wavering into rebellion too."

"I don't know about all that," muttered Douglas. "I just want to get back to somewhere warm, away from this freezing rock."

Haugen gave a deep bark of laughter. "You think

this is cold? Little man, back home this is summer weather."

With that, I dismissed the group and everyone went their own ways. Most grabbed some scran. Dutton turned in for the night. A few of the group played cards, suggested by Schrader, of course. I forbade them to play for real money, though. Haugen and McNulty decided to arm wrestle. Javez was reading a technical manual, Doc was prepping her med kit. Everyone deals with pre-op nerves in their own way. Me? I ran through all the op details again and again in my head, trying to figure out any weak points. No rest for the wicked.

At noon next day we gathered for a final mission briefing and equipment prep. Thirty minutes before zero hour we checked bongos and weapons and began to get suited up. We all wanted to travel as light as we could but no-one wanted to be caught without something useful. Close-range weapons were preferred, SMGs, pistols and knives. Team Red also carried restraint gear, plasticuffs and Doc was packing a sedative she'd prepared for each potential target. It wouldn't knock them out completely. After all who wanted to drag an unconscious body through the snow? But it would take any fight out of the recipient and keep them passive.

With ten minutes to go we ran a final buddy check

and the first two teams set off. Red were to wait for another twenty minutes so that we all reached our IPs at around the same time. I took the opportunity to have another syg before Koenig, Armstrong, Williams and Doc joined me outside and we wound our way through the trenches.

The sentries had been informed of our leaving and saw us over the edge of the forward-most observation pit. From there we ran in a low crouch across open ground before reaching the outer ruins of the Complex. Koenig flashed a red light from his torch three times as we crouched in the cover of half demolished wall. Three flashes came in response from a nearby glassless window in the building directly ahead. Within seconds, a shape loomed out of the dark and beckoned to us, the Rubble Rat assigned to guide us in to the tunnel entrance. No face was visible, the soldier was dressed in a grimy snow suit.

With a gruff "Follow me, keep quiet," the figure turned and noiselessly faded into the gloom.

The moon had risen and reflected brightly off the snow but there were dark pockets of shadow within the ruins and nothing but blackness from the interior of the surviving buildings. The four of us trod carefully as we kept pace with our guide. A few twists and turns, a clamber through a jumble of steel beams and we came to a heavy door set in the side of a large building. The Rat gently tapped a few times and the door opened, also silently, I noticed, I guess a squeaky hinge out here could be a giveaway. Welcome heat rolled out of the doorway and we quickly moved inside. What looked to have once been a factory now played home to one of our forward units.

Cots and sleeping bags were laid out at one end of the room, some occupied. At the other, lit by a string of lamps and gathered around a stove, sat a group of around a dozen figures, all in the same grimy suits as our guide. I noticed that each of them either carried or had a weapon close within reach. Some were drinking from mugs, some chatted quietly, one or two just sat and stared into space. None of them spared us so much as a glance. Our guide barely paused and hurried us across the room, through another door and into a corridor. At the far end of that cold and draughty passageway stood another figure on stag, looking out of the empty window, keeping watch on the threatening darkness beyond. Our guide moved up and whispered to the sentry, before indicating a doorway just before the window. He moved close to me.

"All looks quiet." He said in hushed tones. "Go through that door, bear right, about twenty paces brings you to the tunnel. When you come back make the same signal on your torch, three red, and Rana here will bring you back in."

I touched his shoulder in acknowledgement and we moved to the door. Again, it opened silently and we were once more in the crisp night air, snow crunching underfoot. As they had been here before, the other three led while Doc and I played Arse-end Arnold. Minutes later, we were climbing through an access hatch and down a steel ladder to the tunnel below. Before leaving HQ we had kept a close watch through our surveillance equipment and everything had looked very quiet. We took no chances now though, using our NVGs rather than torches.

We soon got to the spot where the team had previously cleared away rubble, leaving only a thin screen to cover the entrance into the main tunnel. Carefully we moved the screening rubble aside and stealthily trod into the larger network. There was enough clearance here to stand at full height but we all remained in a crouch. Williams took the lead.

Holding up a hand to halt us, he slunk into the darkness. Without a word, each of us had un-slung and readied our firearms. Armstrong tucked a combat knife into his belt. Doc wore a pistol at her hip but carried the medbag that held her syringes at the ready. After a few minutes, Williams returned. We gathered in a huddle while Koenig kept watch on the tunnel.

"All clear ahead," Williams told us. "The main tunnel leads on from here a fair way. However about forty metres up there is a branch to the left. We follow that to the end, then go up, it should bring us out into an engineering plant. We have to assume it's occupied as it's in Spart territory."

I indicated that Williams should lead the way. The tunnel remained clear but we stayed low and made as little noise as possible. Moving into the smaller side tunnel, we eventually came to another metal ladder, leading to a hatchway overhead.

"I'll go," mouthed Koenig. Handing me his SMG, he slowly climbed the ladder. At the top, he carefully turned the wheel and barely lifted the hatch. Taking a look, he opened it wider and beckoned us to follow. We climbed up into a small maintenance room. A bench ran along one side, various tools and pieces of equipment hung on a rack above it. All was dark, all was quiet.

Williams had already moved to the door and cracked it open. Leaving the hatchway open behind us, we followed Williams through the door and into a corridor that took us to a reception area at the front of the building. There was some moonlight coming in from outside, reflecting in sparkles off the broken glass that littered the floor. A desk lay on its side in the corner, the wall behind was pockmarked with bullet holes. We stayed in the shadows and got into a huddle again. This time, Armstrong spoke.

"Okay. According to the Intel, Navarro is working out of a CP in the next building over. We can access it through a rear entry point and be straight in and out. We're hoping that this far back their security will be lax."

"And if it isn't?" asked Koenig.

Armstrong's grin flashed in the moonlight as he brandished his combat knife.

"If it isn't," I interjected, "we withdraw and come back another day. No heroics please!"

We carried out another quick buddy check for loose webbing or equipment. No-one wants to get caught on a door handle as you are rushing out of a place. Doc took up position at the rear of the group, Armstrong led the way and we stepped out into the chill night air. Keeping to shadows we ducked and moved across to the next building. Sure enough, around the corner we found a door, most probably a fire escape. The rest of us kept watch while Armstrong worked a small jemmy bar into the narrow gap between door and frame.

Within seconds, there was a crunch that sounded like a rifle shot in the still air. Without pause, Armstrong swung the door open and entered. We followed, hugging the wall. Armstrong was already on the other side of the room, showing up as a ghostly green figure in my goggles. Through another door, along a short corridor and into a stairwell. Armstrong was there, hand held out in warning. We huddled in again. Armstrong pointed upwards, from where a faint light showed and the echo of music floated down the stairs. I pushed my NVGs up to sit on top of my helmet and the others followed suit.

I nodded to Williams and he carefully placed his SMG on the floor, drawing his pistol and screwing a stubby silencer onto the barrel. He glided up the stairs like a ghost and disappeared from view. There were a tense couple of minutes before we heard a faint cough sound. Seconds later Williams' head and shoulders appeared over the edge of the stairs and he waved us up.

As we got to the next floor, he was dragging a body back into the darkness of the stairs, leaving a faint, bloody smear on the floor. The corridor here was lit with a dull yellow striplight. The stairs continued up above us. Armstrong took a minute to go up and check the landing above. He returned to give us the all clear, so we moved into the corridor itself.

Koenig and Williams were on one side, me and Armstrong on the other. Doc stayed back by the stairs waiting for our call. There were a couple of doors on each side and one at the very end of the corridor. The walls and floor were grey concrete, painted over with that shade of paint I always think of as Institution Green. I didn't know if this was a housing complex for workers or something else but luxury was obviously not a priority for the builders.

The doors along each side were shut, we paused at each to listen briefly. Silence. The music, louder now, was coming from the door ahead. It sounded like some kind of folk music. I'm more of a jazz and blues man myself. Williams and Armstrong covered the doors to the sides, I motioned for Koenig to open the door ahead.

Sometimes you need stealth, other times you just need to go for it. Surprise can be overwhelming and it's often easier to take someone alive by speed than by some tricky manoeuvre. So as soon as Koenig lowered the door handle, I was through, bursting into the room like a bullet. Koenig was immediately behind me and shot down the figure inside who, with lightning reactions, had reached for a gun. As he was flung back against the far wall, the second figure in the room turned to face me. Navarro!

I hurled myself at him, clamping one hand over his mouth and shoving him back against the desk at which he had been sitting. The music came from a small radio on the desk, which was littered with plans and papers. Navarro squirmed beneath my grip, hand moving towards his belt but I banged his head sharply against the wall and he quietened down a bit. By then, Doc was in the room, plunging the syringe into Navarro's arm. I felt him relax beneath me and a beatific smile spread across his face.

"Looks like good shit, Doc," I couldn't help saying. Then, to my prisoner, "Come on, Louka. We are going to meet some friends." I turned to Koenig, "Grab as many of those papers as you can, double quick."

Half marching, half dragging our new friend out of the room we set off back towards the stairs. At that moment a side door opened and a woman came out, straight into Armstrong's knife. With a soft sigh, she sat back into her room, staring in disbelief at the blood that bloomed like a flower across her white vest. Armstrong quietly shut the door and we made it back down the stairs without further incident. We were just at the rear fire exit when the balloon went up. An alarm bell began clanging and we could hear shouts and footsteps from within the building.

I handed Navarro over to Doc.

"Get him to the tunnel, quick! Armstrong, Williams, with Doc, Koenig, with me."

The four of them disappeared, moving fast now that stealth was no longer necessary. I went back to the interior door and opened it a crack. The footsteps were getting louder. I signalled Koenig to leave the room, then unclasped a grenade from my front webbing. Pulling the pin, I rolled it down the corridor, closed the door and made for the exit. A dull boom sounded as I came out of the building, closely followed by a shriek of agony. Glass and snow crunching underfoot, I made the reception area of the first building.

Koenig was waiting there, facing back behind me, SMG raised to his shoulder.

I shouted "Go!" as I reached him and turned to take his place, covering the open space between the buildings.

I hadn't switched back to my NVGs - any kind of flash from a shot or explosion would blind me - but there was enough moonlight outside to make out three or four man sized silhouettes against the snow. I gave them two bursts with the AK before making my own escape. To be on the safe side I dropped a couple more grenades in my wake. I hit the maintenance room as they exploded.

The others were already down the hatch. I followed in short order, pausing only to shut the hatch behind me. No point in leaving a clear trail to follow.

By the time we got to the main tunnel, I had caught the others up. I waved them to go on ahead and crouched silent for a minute, listening for any sounds of pursuit behind us. There was nothing, so I followed the others, catching up with them as they reached the entry tunnel. Doc had already disappeared with Navarro and

Armstrong. Williams and Koenig were replacing what amount of screening rubble they could.

By the time we got back to the Rubble Rats room Doc was already sat drinking a cup of hot soup, while Navarro sat next to her, slack jawed, staring vacantly into the flames of the heater.

Our original guide saw us out to the Complex perimeter before fading away like a phantom and, soon after that, we were back at our bunker. Job done.

CHAPTER 17

THE COMMANDER

I thought it best to keep Navarro with us for what remained of the night. He would be in Happy Land for a few hours yet but he was restrained on a bunk in any case. Before we went out I'd had Schrader return to the Hub to ready the transport and organise an APC for us, which arrived just after dawn. Weaver and Vitali joined me, the prisoner sandwiched in-between them, a bag on his head, hands cuffed behind his back.

Shortly we were back at the Hub, getting Navarro on board *Lady Luck*. Schrader was already in place at the controls.

"All okay?" I clapped him on the shoulder as he flicked switches. Schrader grinned.

"Yep, Skip. Weather is shit as usual but once we're

above this cloud cover we should be alright. I managed to get a transmission through to Kaur upstairs, they're expecting us. I'll pass over our prisoner then head back. Want me to bring anything with?"

"Yes, information, if you can. Slade mentioned hearing something about increased Spart activity, have a nose around see what you can find out."

"Got it, Skip." Schrader returned to his instruments, calling ATC on the "new" old radio fixed to his console.

"*Lady Luck* to Hub Control. Request clearance for take off in ten minutes, over."

The old radio crackled and popped but Control came back straight away.

"Received, *Lady Luck* but please stand by. We have incoming traffic, will advise on take off time. Estimate twenty minutes, over."

Schrader pressed the transmit button again.

"Roger. Standing by, over and out". Then he turned to me again. "More reinforcements coming in?"

I didn't know, so I just shrugged and took my leave. One last check on our prisoner, now bagless and glaring at me, then I hopped out of the ship and headed back into the warm. Vitali and Weaver had gone off to sort out some ammo supplies, so out of courtesy I decided to check in on Colonel Behr, just to apprise him of recent events. He was in his office leafing through reports as I was shown in and he stood to greet me.

"Coffee? Munroe, bring in two coffees, would you?" His aide nodded and left. I filled him on our prisoner and he smiled.

"Good work, one down, two to go!" He rifled through the pile on his desk and pointed to a sheet of paper.

"This came through earlier. It's a report from Captain Gage." At this point the coffee arrived and we sat. Behr nudged the paper across the desk to me. I skimmed it. Insubordination, assault on an officer, failure to comply with orders were just some of the words I saw. I raised my eyebrows at Behr. He smiled and, picking up the paper, stood to feed it into a small machine on his desk.

"Of course," he said, "The problem in a war zone is that communications can very easily go astray."

There was a whirring sound as the paper came out the other end of the machine in little strips, dropping into a waste tray.

"So that is that. Believe me, Gage will soon be too busy to follow up."

"Thank you, sir. I owe you one," I smiled.

Behr waved a hand. "No problem. But listen Naylor, take care. Gage's Uncle, the Senator, is very proud of his nephew being in the Armed Services. You get my drift?"

"Got it, sir."

"Things are changing, Naylor. Like you, I've been out

of the loop for a while but I've been hearing things from the new arrivals about a change of mood back home. These terrorist attacks have everyone on edge. Questions are being asked in the Senate. I've been told there's a cabal of top brass pushing for change. It's bordering on a coup, according to some. Personally I think soldiers should keep out of politics and politicians out of soldiering, but this damned war is having a deeper effect than any of us might have predicted a year ago."

I drained the plastic coffee cup. "Thanks for the heads up. I'll speak to my intel guys and see what they can find out. And yes, I agree, it's like that saying about money being a great servant but a lousy master. The thought of the likes of Gage running the whole show sends a shiver down the spine. Anyway, thanks again sir, I'd best be heading back."

We stood and exchanged salutes, when the door burst open behind me. A tall, slim figure filled the doorway, Munroe's anxious face peering over his shoulder.

"I'm sorry Colonel, this person insisted on-"

The person in question waved a dismissive hand. He was dressed in an immaculate uniform, insignia sparkling in the dim light. A thin, pale face topped with close cropped dark hair surveyed the room as though it were a pigsty. The man peeled off grey, leather gloves and slapped them on the desk.

"Well now, Colonel Behr, I take it? And who might this be?" He examined me as though I were something he'd just found on the sole of his shoe.

I cocked a half-assed salute in his direction.

"Naylor, sir. CO Assault Team 5, currently engaged here on special operations."

For a second, I thought I saw a glimmer of recognition, perhaps even respect in the cold grey eyes. Just for a second.

"If you don't mind me asking," Behr placed both hands on his desk and leaned forward. "Who the hell are you and what do you mean barging into my office like this?"

"As for the who, I am Commander van Vuuren. As for the meaning... why, my dear Behr, I am here to replace you!"

Behr called for more coffee and the three of us sat around like old school chums catching up. Well, not quite. Behr was pissed off. He was hiding it well but I could tell. Van Vuuren seemed vaguely amused by the whole thing. He had asked me to stay as he knew of our mission, it seemed. That filled me with disquiet, for some reason.

"You see gentlemen, the Senate is extremely

concerned about the length of time and amount of resources used in putting down this rebellion. Some are concerned that the war is not being prosecuted fully due to a lack of commitment. You may have heard rumours of an impending change of leadership in government. It is true and you should welcome it, gentlemen, as it consists largely of military leaders, backed by a strong alliance of powerful interests. In short, a group that will give us the strong and stable leadership we need in wartime!"

This was punctuated by another slap on the desk with the gloves. Meanwhile, my mind was racing. Van Vuuren... the name was vaguely familiar. There was an itch at the back of my brain that I couldn't scratch. Behr had a better memory than me. He fixed the Commander with a glare.

"Van Vuuren. The Reber 3 incident last year? You were responsible for the wholesale destruction of the entire rebel colony; men, women and children!"

Van Vuuren inclined his head slightly and smirked.

"Where we have the technology to crush the insurgents, why should we not use it? Please do not tell me your sympathies lie with the rebels, Colonel? It might account for your poor showing here. Back home people are asking whether you are on a military campaign or a winter sports holiday!"

Behr snorted and made to reply but van Vuuren cut him short with a wave of a hand. His expression hardened and his eyes glittered in the dull yellow glow of the striplights.

"I am not interested in your excuses, Behr. Your time here is done." He withdrew an envelope from inside his jacket pocket. "Here is the requisite paperwork. You are to leave on the transport that brought me here. You have precisely one hour to gather your effects and inform your staff."

"My staff, what will - "

"They will be leaving with you. I have brought my own team with me."

Behr opened the envelope and scanned the contents. I caught a glimpse of the header, it was from Supreme Command. Still barely controlling his anger, Behr straightened and snapped off a smart salute.

"Very well, Commander, I shall inform my staff and make preparations to leave immediately."

Van Vuuren stood, casually touched fingers to his forehead in reply and turned to leave. I followed him out, pausing only as Behr muttered to me, "Good luck, Naylor. I think you will need it!"

Van Vuuren was waiting for me in the corridor and swung alongside me as I strode out.

"Well now, Naylor, let us speak candidly. I know of

your background and your mission."

"May I ask how, sir? As far as I was aware this mission was of the highest security level."

The Commander made a casual wave of the hand.

"For the last two years I was on attachment to the DIS. We know everything."

Shit. I masked my distaste and paused, turning towards him.

"Then you will understand my requirement for secrecy, sir, and for the full co-operation of the regular forces here?"

"Indeed, I do, Naylor. And I shall ensure you have both. Should you encounter any difficulties, you are to report to me direct. I will be reviewing and shaking things up here. This rebellion needs to be crushed and I am the man to crush it! Tomorrow I will visit the front line troops. Perhaps you would accompany me?"

I knew it wasn't a request so I had to agree. Arrangements made, I headed back to the APC where the last of the ammo had just been loaded on board. Recent developments aside, it was a glorious day. The sky was a bright, clear cobalt, the sun glinting off the frost and snow. Vitali pointed to the horizon, though, where ominous black clouds stacked up far in the distance, towering high above the open plains. He turned up the collar of his smock and muttered.

"More snow on the way. Heavy stuff, too".

I grinned and slapped him on the back. "Cheerful as ever, Vits. Don't worry, we might be dead tomorrow!"

He grumbled to himself in reply and took his seat in the APC, taking a hefty swig from his hip flask and continuing to mumble. Weaver plonked himself down in the seat next to me and I filled him in on the new command situation. He was as unimpressed by the DIS connection as I was but there was nothing to be done, we had a job to do.

Vitali was right, the temperature dropped sharply that afternoon and there was heavy snowfall overnight. In light of that, I decided to suspend ops for the short term. In any case, the Sparts would be on full alert after last night's incursion. Any thoughts of a quiet day were dispelled by an early morning summons from van Vuuren to meet him immediately. With a sigh I finished my Digger's Breakfast, buttoned up my suit and followed the messenger up to the main CP. As we approached the main entrance, a flustered Sergeant Floyd shot out of the doorway like a bullet, swearing under his breath. Catching my eye he muttered "Fuck this for a game of soldiers!" before stomping off down the trench.

Inside, van Vuuren was already in place, dressed in an immaculate snowsuit. The rest of the staff were stood to attention around the room as though on parade. To my dismay, Gage was there, looking like the cat that got the cream. He glanced over with disgust as I entered. Van Vuuren turned as I came in, stamping my feet and blowing on my hands.

"Ah, here you are Naylor, good! I was just informing this bunch of slackers that things are going to change around here. Correct, Gage?"

I thought Gage was going to burst with excitement. Drawing himself up to his full height, he puffed his chest out and shouted in his best parade ground voice "Yes, sir!"

"Good, good, carry on. Naylor is going to escort me up to the front line."

The radio operator, the only person still sitting as he monitored his set, spoke up.

"Commander, shall I let our units know you are moving up to them?"

"That won't be necessary. I prefer to visit unannounced," Van Vuuren replied.

Gage smirked but the radio op persisted.

"Sir, SOP is to advise all units in the Complex of movements forward, it avoids any misunderstandings or accidents."

Van Vuuren slapped his gloves into his hand. "I said that won't be necessary! I know how this works! You just want to warn them of my inspection so they can tidy up and stop their loafing around! Let me make it clear, if you send any signal I will have you on a charge. Understood?"

"Understood, sir." The radio op look suitably chastened. Well, this was going to be a fun morning.

Van Vuuren buttoned up his smock, put on his gloves, then turned to me. "Naylor, lead on!"

I led the way to the northern jump off point where I had entered the Complex on my first visit. That seemed like a long time ago now. Two figures, swaddled up against the cold and puffing on sygs, manned the observation post. They paid no attention as we entered the emplacement. Van Vuuren stared at them for a few seconds, then began his routine.

"Well? Do you not salute officers here?"

The men glanced round at us and, with puzzled expressions, lifted hands to foreheads. Van Vuuren huffed and moved to look over the lip of the emplacement, forgoing the use of the binos. One of the soldiers coughed.

"Er, I wouldn't advise that, sir. The Spart snipers are very active in this area."

The Commander hesitated, then moved to the binos to peer through them. If his first view of the Complex affected him the same way it had affected me, he didn't show it. He turned away and waved me on. I bade him follow me over the edge, then took him through on the same route I had taken with Fisher's team. I figured it was better to use a known route than try and find my way through that maze of rubble. Besides, it would be a less of a surprise when we arrived - I hoped.

I did take some pleasure in ensuring van Vuuren had to go on his hands and knees and crawl as much as possible. Within a few minutes, his gleaming white suit was stained and damp. We were soon at the ruin where Fisher's team had switched and I thought it best to pause here while I scouted ahead for any of our troops. Van Vuuren nodded agreement and sat, brushing down his muddied snow suit.

I headed off for about five minutes but saw no sign of anyone, so I returned to the Commander and bade him follow me. Not longer after, we were approaching the building opposite the Redhouse. I thought I could move quietly and had good awareness but as we got near to the place a voice came out of the rubble.

"Hold it there, don't move. Go for your gun and you're dead."

We both froze. Two figures rose like spectres training their weapons on us. With a sigh of relief, I saw they had coloured armbands on their right arm. They came closer, one pushing his grimy face close to mine. He had old eyes in a young face. Nodding, he lowered his gun.

"You were here a few days back. You should have told us you were coming in, we could have shot you."

Van Vuuren brushed me aside to confront the Rubble Rat.

"Does no-one here salute their superiors? We are here on my say-so. I am Commander van Vuuren, your new CO. You will take me to your HQ at once!"

The soldier appeared resolutely unimpressed. With a shrug of his shoulders, he nodded to van Vuuren's rank badges.

"I'd remove those if I were you. The last top brass we had out here got nabbed by the Sparts. He screamed all night."

Before van Vuuren could respond, the soldier turned and bade us follow. Crouching low, working round the side of the ruin and moving slowly, we soon reached a second stag point. Not long after that, we were escorted through a doorway, down a corridor and into a large open space inside a building. Van Vuuren strode in like a conquering hero, to be greeted by a wave of indifference. I thought he was going to blow a gasket.

"Who is the senior officer here!" he thundered. A hulking shape in the corner, syg clenched between teeth that shone white in a smoke blackened face, looked up from the hand of cards he was holding.

"Who's asking?" he growled.

The Commander strolled over, peeling off his gloves, towards the figure who had already turned back to his card game. For a horrible moment, I thought he was going to slap the soldier with his gloves but, thankfully he restrained himself.

"Stand up, soldier! I am Commander van Vuuren, your new CO! I am here to inspect your troops and your positions. Report!"

The grizzled figure slowly stood, turned and spat out his syg. Touching a gloved hand to the peak of his cap he threw his shoulders back and yelled. "Sergeant Mayne, sir. Currently on standby awaiting the return of the boss, er, of the CO, sir."

Van Vuuren inspected the man as though he were a lab specimen.

"Look at the state of you, Mayne! It's a disgrace! Where are your rank badges!"

Mayne looked at the Commander as though he were mad. "We remove them, sir. We found the Spart snipers and snatch teams were targeting officers."

"I see. Scared of some ragtag rebel scum, are we? And why are you scratching yourself man?"

Mayne grinned. "That would be the lice, sir, little buggers they are. Some are of the opinion that they work for the Sparts. My view is they'll have a bite on anyone. Even officers."

Van Vuuren grimaced and took a step back. "And your CO, where is he?"

"She, sir. She took a team out earlier to recover some of wounded from a patrol that was ambushed this morning. I expect - ah, here she is now."

The heavy main door burst open and in strode Yao. Slinging her assault rifle over her back, she removed her helmet, tossed it aside and moved towards the large heater in the centre of the room, shaking her head. She put her hands towards the heater, exclaiming loudly "It's colder than a witch's tit out there! Franks, there's three wounded coming in, see to them will you." Then she caught sight of the Commander and me, stood like a spare one next to him.

"Well, well, Mr Observer, and you have brought a friend with you?"

I did my best to look apologetic, van Vuuren was already on the move. Yao quickly sized him up, noting his uniform insignia and my desperate eyebrow waggling. She straightened up and snapped off a salute.

"Lieutenant Yao, sir. Acting CO, 2nd Battalion."

"A Lieutenant commanding a battalion?"

"Yes, sir. I'm the most senior officer in the field. The rest were, well, killed or captured, sir"

Van Vuuren considered this for a moment, then drew

himself up to his full height and planted his feet apart, hands behind his back.

"Yao, this is a shambles. Your troops look like tramps. There is a conspicuous absence of discipline here and I fail to see why a Terran Alliance military unit is struggling so much against a bunch of mine workers!"

"Sir, if I may -" proffered Yao.

"No, you may not!" The Commander shouted in her face. I noticed a subtle shift in the troops sat around the room. More than one hand dropped to a sidearm. Van Vuuren, oblivious, continued.

"I want an immediate roll call, I want all your troops gathered here for inspection within ten minutes!"

Yao looked stunned.

"But sir, we have units out on patrol. We have units guarding key points. To call them back in would be to surrender vital points we have spent weeks fighting over!"

I saw the flash of defiance in her eyes and caught, again, the movement of some of her troops. Van Vuuren was having none of it and thrust his face closer towards Yao's.

There are moments in any conflict when the Gods of War smile upon you. This was one of those occasions, though unpleasant enough in its own way. The building shook as a loud explosion sounded outside. Concrete dust fell from the ceiling, adding to the mess on van Vuuren's uniform. A voice from the doorway cried "Sparts! Spart attack!" and there was a nearby burst of SMG fire.

Yao was on it instantly. She grabbed the goggle-eyed van Vuuren and pushed him towards Mayne.

"Get him out of here!" she snapped. "Back way! Squad Three, on me! Squad Two, up the stairs. Vasquez, see who you can raise on the radio, some mortar support would be welcome!"

She retrieved her helmet from the floor and, buckling up the chinstrap looked at me. "You'd best go with his nibs, if the Sparts caught our CO ..."

I nodded. "Will do. And take care, alright?"

She smiled, ratched back the bolt on her AR and disappeared through the large doorway. Mayne had the Commander by the scruff of his smock and was dragging him away through another doorway. I followed, flicking the safety off my AK.

We moved quickly through a series of rooms to an external door. Mayne pushed it open a crack and peered out. After listening, he opened the door wider and went through, beckoning us to follow. He had let go of van Vuuren by now, who had drawn his own pistol and, to his credit, didn't look the least bit afraid. A burst of fire rattled above our head and Mayne spun and returned fire. A figure flung its hands up and toppled down a pile of rubble to our right.

Mayne held up a hand and we crouched, breath smoking in the freezing air. Mayne motioned for me to move left and I saw his plan immediately. With a brief "Stay here!" to the Commander, I doubled forward at a crouch, moving around the edge of the rubble. Sure enough, my movement caused another figure to pop its head up and raise a gun, only to fall back from Mayne's head shot. Without pause I continued to the other side of the rubble, giving a burst from the hip at the two remaining Sparts stood there.

I gave Mayne a whistle and he appeared with the CO in tow. He took the lead again; me, I was lost in this bloody nightmare maze. Through another building, a sprint across an open street and then the Redhouse loomed ahead. I nudged Mayne as he crouched peering round a corner.

"I can take it from here, I know where we are now."

Mayne nodded and muttered, "Good luck!" before loading another mag into his SMG and disappearing back into the snow-covered ruins.

"Follow me now, sir," I advised van Vuuren. He stuck close by me as we approached the ruin. S o m e t h i n g wasn't right. Call it soldier's intuition, call it what you will, but as we approached the building I caught a glimpse of movement. I was in no mood to take chances, I pulled the pin out of a grenade and flung it through the nearest window. As soon as it exploded I was through the door, spraying the room as I went in. The Commander was close behind, so close he bumped into me, making me almost trip over the bodies at my feet. Two of them, shredded to pieces by the frags and bullets. By some chance the face of one was undamaged, a young lad, perhaps in his late teens, gun still clasped in hand. Van Vuuren swallowed hard and quickly averted his gaze. I guess seeing the results of your handiwork up close is a different experience from launching an orbital nuke.

However, the way was now clear and we were soon heading back to the trench system. Before we got there, van Vuuren bid me halt, and we hunkered down behind a rusted water tank.

"Thank you, Naylor, for what you did back there."

I shrugged. It was my job after all, and to lose a CO out in the field was not a smart career move. On the other hand, having the gratitude of a CO, a DIS one at that, was no bad thing.

"I gather you have experienced some personal issues with Captain Gage?" he added. I nodded.

"You must be patient with him, Naylor. I know his Uncle well. We were at the Academy together."

That figured, I thought but kept it to myself. Then

came the sales pitch. I had been expecting it since our meeting yesterday, to be honest, I had guessed what was coming.

"In any case, best keep clear of him. I will see to it that he doesn't interfere with your operation. But that is not the main issue, Naylor. Times are changing. We are poised to take control of the Senate."

"We, sir?"

"The military, Naylor. People of insight and determination. People who understand what needs to be done, who are ready to take the action required to deal with…" he waved a hand around. "With all this."

"I see, sir, but what does this have to do with me?"

"You're an experienced and respected solider, Naylor, the same goes for the rest of your unit. Other personnel look up to you, they will follow your lead. Do you understand?"

I understood perfectly but sometimes it pays to act dumb.

"Sorry, sir, I don't. I'm just here to do my job."

"Precisely, Naylor. But what is that job and how far will you go to accomplish it? I'm not asking you to do much, just be aware that certain elements who oppose our group may need to be neutralised."

"Neutralised, sir?" I knew I was over-egging the dumb routine but I was stalling for time. What could I say? Stick it up your arse, sir? Part of me wondered if I should just shoot him on the spot and claim a sniper got him.

As it happened, the cavalry arrived, in the form of today's replacement squad heading out into the Complex. Fisher was leading them and he grinned as he saw me. I noticed the group with him were all considerably cleaner than the previous time. He picked up on my look.

"Newbies," he explained, " I'm taking them up to see the big bad Sparts."

Then he turned to van Vuuren, saluting.

"Commander? Captain Gage said I might find you out here. He said to return immediately, there is some kind of flap on at The Hub. I'll have one of the men here see you back in, our look outs are a little jumpy this morning."

With that he and his team faded into the rubble. The soldier left with us saluted and we turned back towards our lines. Nothing more was said, though before we parted van Vuuren grasped my arm.

"Think on it, Naylor," he whispered "But not for long. Things are moving quickly and those not with us…"

He left the threat hanging in the cold air along with his breath and disappeared along the trench.

CHAPTER 18

THE ATTACK

Heavy snow set in again the next afternoon, the wind driving it in stinging, almost horizontal lines across the open plain. We huddled up in the bunker, there seemed little point doing anything else. As darkness fell, the storm eased off. Pops and I decided to stretch our legs along the trench. I wanted to talk to him about van Vuuren's little sales pitch yesterday without involving the rest of the team. He'd had far more experience dealing with higher-ups and their power games than me. We headed up to one of the front line OPs and I told the soldier on watch to get back inside and grab some grub. She gratefully saluted and hurried off in the gloom. Pops flashed the sygs, I broke out a thermos and we settled down to chat.

"So, you remember the DIS?" I asked him.

Pops exhaled blue smoke and scowled. "Hard to forget those arseholes."

"Well, there's good news and bad news."

"Go on," he prompted.

"The good news is, they like us. The bad news, they are here. The new CO, van Vuuren, is direct from DIS."

"Van Vuuren?" Pops grimaced even more. "Our new CO? Shit, that's not good. The man's a fanatic. You know he was responsible for nuking a whole colony? It was hushed up but - "

Pops was interrupted by a sound like bed sheets tearing, followed by a scream from Hell itself. The whole trench line shuddered as we came under a rocket barrage. We both immediately dropped into the slush as the twilight was lit by orange and red flashes. The enemy had the range perfect, the bombardment landed square on our leading lines and emplacements. The air was filled with the smell of cordite and red-hot shards of shrapnel whizzed overhead. After about five minutes, there was a short pause in the maelstrom, Pops took advantage of it to take a look through the binos.

"There's people out there, moving towards us." He squinted into the darkness again. "Can't tell who they are, but they are heading this way."   Without a word, we prepped our weapons. Along the trench there were screams of the wounded and a klaxon blared out. Three soldiers rushed into the emplacement, manhandling a gimpy into place. An expectant hush fell over the whole sector, broken only by the hiss of a star shell soaring up and out over the wasteland ahead. In its white glare I could see figures approaching, moving awkwardly through the snow. The bolt of the gimpy clunked back, the team preparing to shoot, when a voice shouted through the dark.

"Hold your fire! They're ours!"

There was a drumming of footsteps from ahead, then bodies began dropping over the lip of the trench and into the emplacement. Rubble Rats. An SMG barked out into the darkness, followed by more shouts. Tracer fire whipped overhead. The Rats immediately began taking up positions, I could see more of them jumping in all along the sector. One final figure leaped in, almost knocking me over. A familiar voice cursed in the dark. It was Yao.

"Mr Obs! We must stop meeting like this!"

I grinned, then motioned back towards the Complex. "What's happening?"

"Sparts. Scores of them. We had to conduct a fighting retreat through the Complex. Their numbers are overwhelming, I don't know where the fuck they came from but they are heading this way!"

Shouldering her AR, she took a place on the emplacement edge. Sporadic fire was breaking out along the line, though I could see nothing moving out front yet.

Then I saw them, a line of hunched shapes. They came in like a wave, firing from the hip. Just to round things off, the rockets started again, arcing over us to hit our rear lines. Immediately our front line burst into return fire, tracer and bullets whistling across the wasteland. Many of the attackers dropped in that murderous hail of fire but many more kept coming. There was a dull plopping sound and whistles, then more shells arced in to burst on our trench line. Not explosives this time, but smoke. Luckily for us, someone over there had mistimed the barrage. Five minutes earlier and we would have been blind to the attackers. As it was, we at least put a dent in their first wave.

The smoke stung like hell and cut vision down to a couple of metres. Dense and white, it hung heavy in the air. Bullets continued to whip overhead. There was a sudden shout as enemy appeared on the lip of the emplacement. Yao shot two down with a sweep of her rifle, but three more dropped into the trench. I turned to find myself staring down the barrel of an SMG. Before he could fire, the Spart pointing it gave a high pitched scream and collapsed to the floor, revealing a grim faced

Pops behind him, bloody knife in hand. There was no time for thanks as more figures tumbled in on top of us.

I can't remember much of what happened next. Just confused impressions of scrabbling in the slush, of a grimacing face above me, of fingers gripped around my throat as I stabbed and stabbed with my knife. Getting to my knees I saw Pops with a Spart sat astride him, his knife hand pinned while he held his attacker's knife hand in a grip to stop him stabbing down. Yao suddenly loomed behind, placed the muzzle of her pistol to the Spart's ear and calmly blew half his head away. In doing so she turned her back on another Spart who brutally clubbed her with the butt of his rifle, knocking Yao to her knees. That gave me the opening I needed and with a swift overarm throw I buried my knife in the man's chest. Pops finished the job by sweeping the Spart's feet from under him and stabbing him twice. He pulled out my knife and tossed it back to me.

I rushed to Yao as she stood, face clenched in pain.

"Are you hurt?" I asked.

"My shoulder aches like hell, whole arm is numb."

"Stick close, let's get you to a medic."

There were no live Sparts left in the emplacement, though we could hear shouts and the chatter of guns through the smoke. A soldier suddenly burst in behind us, breathless.

"Everyone pull back, we're bringing artillery fire down on the forward trench line!"

We needed no further prompting, pulling Yao and another wounded soldier with us we got out quick sharp, heading back towards the second line. None to soon either, as shells whistled in low, wreathing the front line in a wall of fire. Someone upstairs was on the ball it seemed!

I saw Yao to the nearest med post then set off up to the main CP to try and get an idea of what was happening. There was sentry on the door this time, he let me through with a nod. Inside, Gage was striding up and down, pale faced, goggle-eyed, mud all down one side of his snow suit. Sergeant Floyd noticed me and came over grinning.

"Is he alright?" I asked, nodding towards Gage.

"He was out on the front line when the attack came in. Some Sparts shot at him, I think he's taking it personally."

I smiled. "Still, he called that artillery strike in, that was quick thinking."

"Actually that was me, sir." Floyd looked sheepish. "The Captain was, er, not quite himself at the time so I took the initiative."

I shook my head. "Good work, Floyd. So what's going

on now?"

"Call has gone back to HQ, the Commander is on the way in. In the meantime, it looks like our artillery strike broke the back of the attack, reports are that the Sparts have retreated back into the Complex."

"For how long, I wonder? Okay, I'd best speak to Gage, then I'll head back to check on the team. Let me know if there's anything I can do."

Floyd nodded and went out the door. I walked over to Gage, the man looked terrified and was babbling orders constantly. Luckily, the radio staff was an old hand and knew to ignore him. I stood in front of the Captain and snapped off a salute.

"Naylor, sir, reporting in. Is there anything we can do?"

Gage noticed me for the first time and returned the salute with a shaky hand.

"Naylor! What the, my God, there were so many of them, explosions, shooting, I..."

You feel for anyone after their first time in action but frankly this was embarrassing. The rest of the staff were quietly going about their jobs, taking in reports, coordinating a response. Thank God Floyd had been here to take charge. There was nothing I could do here, so I sat Gage down and poured him a stiff drink from the bottle of scotch on his desk. Then, knowing van Vuuren was on the way, I decided to be elsewhere.

I caught up with Yao at the med station, she had her arm in a sling.

"Possible fracture," she said.

"Does it hurt?" I smiled.

"Only when I laugh," she smiled back

"I won't tell you my best joke then, However, I can offer some anesthetic?" I pulled the bottle of scotch out of my jacket and raised my eyebrows.

"You never told me you were a medic, Mr Obs? What other talents do you have?"

"Let's find somewhere quiet to finish this off and I'll show you my party piece."

Yao laughed, then winced and indicated I should lead on. My room back at the bunker was reasonably private. Well, about a private as you can get in a war-zone. Most of the rest of the team were sat around the main room, and, bless them, none of them so much as batted an eyelid as the pair of us came in and disappeared through the curtained doorway.

The next morning I woke with a hangover but also some pleasant memories. Yao had already left, the army makes no concessions for romance. No doubt she would have been called in to make a full report to van Vuuren. Everyone was up and about, eating breakfast, cleaning gear or, in Javez' case checking signals from our surveillance equipment.

"Nothing," she told me. "It's probably best to assume that all the tunnel entrances are compromised."

"That makes life difficult." Kuruk wandered over, coffee in hand. "Without eyes, it's risky going back in that way again."

"Agreed" I helped myself from the coffee pot and called everyone round for a conflab.

Taking into account the info from Javez and the considerable increase in Spart manpower, we had to come up with a new strategy if we were to complete the mission. Koenig wondered if we could go undercover and infiltrate the Sparts. Weaver pointed out that with the new influx of troops we would stand a better chance, new faces wouldn't stand out so much.

Pops agreed but pointed out the attendant risks. Following our previous grab, the Sparts would be on high alert for a similar operation. Also, it's one thing to be caught in open battle, or even a stealth mission, but working undercover is a whole different ball game. We would have to be operating at peak capacity. I told the team I'd think on it and, if there were no other suggestions, make a decision later that day.

About that time, Schrader returned, back from his trip upstairs. He handed out a few bits and pieces that he'd promised to bring back; vodka for Vitali, a carton of chocolate for Haugen and a fancy, scented envelope for Pops.

"Who on Earth's that from? You got a fancy lady upstairs?" asked Koenig.

"Never you mind!" replied Pops, tapping the side of his nose before going off somewhere quiet to read his letter.

Schrader sat down at the table with the rest of us and gave us the news while helping himself to some breakfast.

"There's a major flap on upstairs. The Navy bods are buzzing around like blue-arsed flies." He paused to take a mouthful of beans. "There's Spart activity all through the system, FTL ships popping in and out. From the intel coming in, it looks like the Sparts have put in a big crowd of reinforcements at the Complex. Hundreds, perhaps."

I grimaced. "Oh yes, we met some of them last night."

Schrader shrugged and took another mouthful.

"That's not all. I spoke to a pal of Slade's up there. There are indications that the Sparts are also moving in heavy engineering equipment."

"What for? And where's it going?" I asked.

"I don't think it's going into the Complex," Kuruk

ventured. "At least, I've heard nothing about it from our contact. And heavy plant would be difficult to hide."

"Okay. Can you try and contact him today, see if he has anything new? Also run through the undercover idea with him, I'd like his take on it."

Kuruk nodded. "I'll see what I can do."

I turned back to Schrader. "Anything else?"

"Yes." He wiped his mouth on a paper napkin. "All the troops that went back upstairs are being recalled in the light of last night's attack."

I whistled. "Wow. They won't be happy. Just when they thought they were out."

"They pulled me back in!" said Slade in some weird accent. "Sorry, Skip," he grinned. "It's from an old movie."

Javez threw a glove at his head, Slade dodged it, then stood to take his plate over to the kitchen area. The glove bounced of Haugen's arm, he paused from munching his chocolate to look up and shake his head.

I clapped our flyboy on the shoulder.

"Okay, thanks, Schrader. Get some kip if you like, I won't need you for the rest of the day.

With a "Cheers, Skip," he headed off and I sat down with another coffee to think.

A little later that morning, one of Floyd's team popped his head in to let me know there was a big conflab going on at the CP. I didn't relish the thought of seeing van Vuuren again but it was important we knew what was happening operationally. I grabbed Vitali and Kuruk and we headed to the CP. Fortunately the Commander had been and gone, Gage was now running the show. We settled in unnoticed at the back to enjoy the performance.

It seemed that the attack last night had fallen solely on our southern sector. Gage was insisting this showed poor tactics and planning on behalf of the Sparts. Kuruk coughed and raised his hand.

"Excuse me, sir but there is another explanation." Gage looked taken aback and Kuruk gave him no chance to respond, pressing on quickly with his theory.

"It seems more likely to me that the attack was a diversion. They came forward in numbers but not in any real focused way. They also retreated quickly, considering they had reached our forward lines. The question is, a diversion for what?"

By now Gage had recovered his poise and struck what he no doubt thought was a commanding pose.

"Well, that's all well and good, er... chappy, but a little far-fetched. These are rebel miners we are facing, not highly-trained troops, I think we can discount your theory, entertaining as it is."

"Rebel miners who have held our forces here in

deadlock for months," Kuruk responded. A hush fell over the room. Then a voice spoke from the corner.

"Captain, we have reports that three of our sentries in the northern sector are missing."

Gage bridled at the comment.

"In my experience, sentries go "missing" all the time." He even did the little quote thing with his fingers. "Most likely they have skipped duty to get back in the warm somewhere. Also, some bolt and hide at the first whiff of trouble!"

Vitali snorted. "Yes, and some shit their pants and fall apart under fire."

Gage flushed red as a ripple of laughter rolled around the room. I tried hard to stop a grin and gave Vits a sharp kick on the leg. Too late, the damage was done. Gage cast a furious glance at Vitali, then at me.

"Sergeant, I suggest you keep your men under control!"

There was nothing he could do and he knew it. He turned back to the ops map.

"As you heard earlier, the Commander has recalled all troops who were recently relieved. They will begin taking up positions again later today. With our numbers boosted, tomorrow we will strike back against the enemy with a bold thrust into the heart of the Complex!"

Kuruk shook his head and whispered to me. "With

this idiot in charge we have no chance of infiltration. I suggest we consider pulling out."

I agreed. "Okay. But I'd like to have one more look tonight, before the Galloping Major there storms in. We don't know for sure that the tunnels were discovered, let's at least have a looksee."

Kuruk and Vitali nodded and as Gage continued expounding his grand strategy, I caught Sergeant Floyd's eye. I filled him in quietly on our plans and he told us he would let the troops in our approach sectors know that we were moving in and out.

That night, once again I found myself crouching in the snow, cold biting into my bones despite the snow suit. I was with Team Red and we were on the approach to the tunnel we'd previously used. Some of our forces had gone back into the Complex outskirts and they loomed out of the darkness at our RV to guide us in to the tunnel entrance.

Team Blue were out to the north of us, acting as a a screen. Team White, with Kuruk in tow, were on a different mission altogether. Kuruk had received word from his brother that he wanted out. Things were getting too hot for him, so he'd made the decision to abort and extricate. Team White were going in to pick him up and escort him safely back across our lines.

Moving quietly, we pushed on and were soon in the tunnel. Everything was as quiet as before so we moved up to the access point. Koenig pointed to the surveillance devices, all still in place. We turned our attention to the rubble screen. It also looked undisturbed.

Moving up to it, I was about to remove a brick when Williams grabbed my arm in a strong grip. I turned to look at him and he pointed slowly. Just by the brick, barely visible in the gloom, was a wire. Shit, a booby trap. Exhaling slowly, I signalled for us all to move back. Two of the team swung their lights down to check the ground around us. Luckily it all seemed clear.

We moved halfway back up the tunnel and stopped for a conflab. It was clear that this route was monitored and, even if we got through the trap, we would most likely find bigger trouble further on. With regret, I signalled for us to head back to our lines. Our Rubble Rat guide was still in place at the tunnel entrance and, pausing only to contact Team Blue, we made our way back to the trenches.

Approaching, we let off a signal flare and gave the agreed password as we came in. Within minutes, we were over the lip of the trench and swigging hot drinks. About five minutes later there was another flare and Team Blue dropped into the emplacement, rubbing hands and stamping feet.

I was explaining the situation to them when another flare went up further up the trench line. It was followed by the chatter of a machine gun, one of ours from the sound of it. We were all instantly on alert but not thinking too much more about it. Then McNulty asked, "Isn't that where Team White are coming back in?"

With an oath, I threw down my coffee and raced through the trench line towards the noise, the rest following behind. A couple of minutes later I burst into the forward emplacement, manned by a two man gimpy crew, stood over by Captain Gage. The gunner had stopped firing and looked at Gage questioningly. Gage shouted at the man.

"I didn't tell you to stop, keep firing, man, it's an attack I tell you!"

The gunner hesitated, then turned back to his gun.

"Belay that order!" I shouted. "That's our team out there!"

The gunner paused, looking at Gage, then at me.

"Fire, damn you!" Gage hissed, hand falling to his holster. By now, the rest of the group were in the emplacement. From out ahead I could hear Vitali's voice, shouting the password.

"Fire and you're dead!" snarled Khan, pointing his SMG at the unfortunate gunner. Gage turned as if to protest but I grabbed the front of his jacket and flung him aside.

"Get out there, help them!" I barked and McNulty, Dutton and Williams immediately went over the top. Khan kept his SMG trained on the gunner. Koenig, seeing that Gage still had his hand on his holster, yanked him back off his feet and, in one smooth move, removed Gage's pistol and threw it off into the dark.

"We have wounded!" came a cry from out front. Armstrong turned, "I'll get medics." and darted back into the trenches.

Then the rest of the team out front appeared, dragging and carrying some of their number. In the meantime, the gunner was jabbering.

"I told him it was our people but the Captain insisted I shoot! He said it was an attack, like last night. He ordered me to shoot!"

"Shut up!" I snapped then focused on helping the in-comers over the edge. Weaver came in first, eyes flashing in the dark.

"Who the fuck opened fire on us?" he growled.

Next, McNulty and Dutton manhandled the huge bulk of Haugen in. His face was porcelain white, his breathing loud and ragged. Blood stained the side of his snowsuit. Vitali, helped by Williams, was in next, face crumpled in pain, clutching his shoulder. Finally came Kuruk, stumbling as he half-dragged, half-carried a figure in a padded khaki suit. Across the chest was stitched a neat line of bloody bullet holes. McNulty and Koenig jumped out to help him and brought the slumped figure in, laying it down on the duckboards. Kuruk kneeled at its side, loosening the clothing and desperately feeling for a pulse.

"Mirek! Mirek!" he cried, turning into sobs as the sightless eyes rolled back in their sockets. Weaver placed a hand on Kuruk's shoulder and said quietly, "He's gone."

Kuruk rocked back on his heels, then looked up, directly at Gage.

"You bastard, you killed my brother," he whispered.

You could never call Kuruk a scary man but at that moment he exuded such menace that every person there shifted a step back. The gunner was trying to make himself as small as possible in the corner. Gage, on his feet again, wiped at the trickle of blood from his nose. He knew he was close to death but still attempted to justify his actions, whining "I wasn't told of any operation, I didn't know it was your team, I thought it was another attack."

"You bastard, you killed my brother!" Kuruk was standing now and a knife had appeared in his hand. Gage edged back until he came up against the sandbagged wall, his palms raised up as if appealing for mercy. Kuruk advanced.

Would I have stopped him? I don't know. Maybe Gage really didn't know about the operation. Maybe he saw a chance for revenge. Maybe he was just scared stupid. Whichever it was, the decision was taken out of my hands when Armstrong burst in with Doc and a med team.

I grabbed Kuruk sharply and our priority became the wounded. We assisted the meds in getting our people onto stretchers, Gage taking the opportunity to slink away. The gunner and his mate, both white as a sheet, said nothing. Khan flung an oath at them before we left ourselves, heading back to the bunker.

CHAPTER 19

THE STATION

ater, we were sat in our main room, each of us wrapped in their own thoughts. Vitali's wound had been dressed and he'd discharged himself from the Medbay. He sat bandaged and still, nursing a vodka. Doc fussed around him a little, offering him some painkillers but he declined and nodded towards the bottle in front of him.

"I have painkiller."

Kuruk sat motionless. He hadn't said a word since returning from the Medbay, where his brother's body now lay. Kahn offered him some food and drink but Kuruk simply turned away. Weaver came into the dugout, he had stayed with the wounded. He stamped snow off his boots and moved towards the stove.

"Haugen is in a bad way. He took three to the gut. They are moving him up to the Hub to ready him for medevac. They have better facilities upstairs."

"And Gage?" I asked.

"No sign of him, Skip. I expect he has found a hole to crawl into somewhere."

Adding to the gloom was the fact we'd have to abort the mission. None of us liked leaving a job half done. And considering tonight's events, we felt we had little to show for our efforts. Slade and Javez had already started to clear away the maps and charts. I told everyone to be ready to move out in the morning.

It was a quiet group that sat in the APC on the drive back up to the Hub. Kuruk remained totally withdrawn, not surprising in the circumstances I suppose. Our progress seemed very slow, confirmed when the driver looked over his shoulder to address us.

"We are being asked to pull over to let oncoming traffic get through. Must be all the troops returning from upstairs."

"How far are we from the Station?" I asked.

"It's just up ahead."

"Okay, pull in there and we'll hold until the road is clear."

Within a few minutes, we were travelling up the slip

ramp and came to a halt in the main Station parking area. I signalled to the team to stretch their legs, have a piss, grab a coffee. Everyone nodded except Kuruk. Doc gently took his arm and looked at me, mouthing "I'll take him."

She led him up and out of the APC and across to the nearby service buildings. The rest of the team did likewise, apart from Dutton, snoring loudly in his seat. None of us had the heart to wake him, so we left him in peace.

Pops and Slade joined me in the outdoor smoking area for a syg. From there we could see the main road, both lanes filled with slow moving trucks heading to the Complex. Fortunately the weather had cleared, the sky was bright blue, the sunlight dazzling off of the snow.

We had just finished our sygs and turned to go back inside, when a volley of shots rang out close by. At once we unslung weapons and moved towards the source of the noise. Rounding the far side of the building, we came upon a strange scene. Six bodies lay sprawled at the foot of the building wall. Blood slowly stained the white snow red as it spread from the bodies. An officer stood over them, pistol in hand. As we watched, he raised the gun and shot one of the figures on the ground. A few metres away stood a group of soldiers, rifles lowered, shifting uneasily.

I strode towards the officer, a Lieutenant I saw from his crisp uniform. My hand hovered on the trigger guard of my AK.

"What's going on here?" I asked. The officer looked up, pistol still in hand.

"Who are you to ask?" His face was lean and scarred, burn marks from the look of it down one cheek.

"Naylor, Assault Team Five, sir."

The officer holstered his weapon. "Ah, the bold Naylor. Yes, the Commander has told me all about you. I'm Lieutenant Webb, Security Adviser to Commander van Vuuren."

"And these people?" I gestured to the bodies, male and female, mostly young.

"Rebel scum captured in the recent attack. Having ascertained they had no intelligence value, I decided to dispose of them. Commander's orders."

"You shot them?" Slade narrowed his eyes. "In cold blood?"

"What would you have me do with them? Resources are limited." He gestured to a nearby building. "Our interrogation facility has little in the way of amenities for prisoners. And they are rebels, it is no more than they deserve."

I was about to make another comment when a distant sound caught our ears. It was a kind of throbbing sound, up in the air somewhere. A dull *whack-whack-whack*, steadily growing louder. Then, beneath it, the hum of engines. Slade looked up, puzzled.

"That sounds like helicopters!"

"What?" I said.

"Helicopters. Choppers. 20th century, rotor blade machines. Sounds like Apocalypse Now!"

I didn't understand the reference but the apocalypse part proved right. Windscreens glinting silver in the sun, a row of machines appeared low in the sky, approaching from the north. They were about twenty metres up, two lines of them, five in each line. All around us, people were looking up to watch their approach. Something didn't feel right. As far as I knew, we had no aerial units in the area, but then neither did the Sparts.

For what use it might be, I raised the AK. Others obviously felt the same, the noise drawing people from outside the main building, some unslinging rifles. Pops nudged me. "I think we should get under cover".

We had just begun to move when, with a roar, the machines surged forward, splitting left and right, noses dipping down. At once there was the hiss of rockets, followed by machine gun fire, as the choppers began attacking the traffic on the road. Within seconds, half a dozen trucks were burning, another two exploded into fragments, leaving little more than scorch marks on the tarmac.

The choppers obviously had plan. The two groups worked east and west along the road, then turned back for a second strafing run. Shouts filled the air, cries of alarm, barked orders and the yells of the wounded. A figure, ablaze from head to foot, ran screaming along the road before mercifully being mowed down by gunfire from above. Everywhere, troops were spilling out of lorries and buildings, raising weapons to the sky and firing in confusion and anger at the machines that buzzed like angry insects overhead.

Work done on the convoy, one group next turned their attention to the Station. The chaos now spread directly around us. The three of us sprinted and dived into a nearby ditch. Rockets came screaming in to hit the buildings, there was a crump of explosions and smoke and dust soon filled the cold air. I saw a group of troops out in the open take aim at the choppers, a line of chain gun bullets cut them down like a scythe. There were more explosions, then suddenly the machines were gone, the sound of their blades fading in the cold, morning air.

They left behind a scene of devastation. The highway was a mass of burning wreckage and bodies. The Station had taken a pounding, half the buildings were on fire. We made our way back towards the parking area, to meet the rest of the team staggering, coughing and spluttering.

A quick head count and I could see everyone was okay. Then Khan nudged me.

"Shit, Skipper. Dutton!" He pointed to our APC, it was burning furiously, a direct hit from the look of it.

"Fuck!" I shouted, racing over, the rest close behind. To no avail, nothing could survive that inferno. The driver, Dutton, both gone, plus half our gear! The team stood around helpless, moving back as ammo started to pop in the wreckage. A few of us retched at the smell of burning flesh and plastic, the knowledge that it was our colleague in there was sickening.

Webb brought us back to the present. Striding over, he took control.

"Naylor! Gather your people and set up a security perimeter. You!" He motioned to a group of troops stood stunned nearby. "Begin gathering the wounded. Place them in the Med Centre!"

There was a *whump* as an ammo truck exploded on the road. Webb swore under his breath and asked me to accompany him. Leaving the rest of the team to secure the area, I followed the Lieutenant to the building he had previously pointed out. I didn't know what the place's original purpose was, but he had turned into a CP come interrogation centre. A radio operator rushed up, handing him a sheet of paper. Webb swore again.

"It looks like this is only part of a greater attack. The

Hub is under assault from large forces, attacking from north and south. Aerial assault as well as ground forces. Where the hell did they come from?" We moved into an office and Webb sat on the desk.

"The Commander has ordered me to gather my staff and return back up the road to the Hub. I have no orders for you or your team, in absence of which I would request that you stay here and keep the Station secure. We do not know if rebel ground forces are on the way. It is vital the Highway remain open and in our hands!"

"Very well, sir." I figured staying here was better than being dragged off with this lunatic.

"There are some supplies and ammo in our building here, scrape together what and who you can. Hold here until further orders, clear?"

"Clear, sir." With that, he exited the room, shouting for his staff. I made my way back outside to deliver the good news.

A couple of hours later I had gathered together the remaining personnel, allocated what weapons and ammo we had to hand, and set up a defensive perimeter. Webb had taken his radio man with him, but we had a coms room at the Station which, fortunately, had escaped the worst of the damage.

More troops came in later, reporting that they'd heard heavy artillery fire from the direction of the Complex. We also saw and heard those choppers again, in the distance, travelling west. My guess was a coordinated attack from each end of the Highway, plus that strafing run. Right now, we were having little luck raising anyone on the comsnet. It was flaky at the best of times, so whether it was down to atmospherics or enemy action, I couldn't say.

On the plus side we were, for the moment at least, warm and reasonably secure in what buildings were still usable. The Station had a good amount of provisions laid in, so we weren't about to starve to death. The position was not particularly strong from a defensive point of view but very little was out here on the broad, empty plains. The best I could do was post lookouts, though they had to be relieved every thirty minutes in this cold.

I gathered together all available officers and NCOs for a conflab. The first question on everybody's lips was "Where the fuck did that come from?"

It was Kuruk who came through with the answer. For the first time since his brother's death he spoke up.

"The Sparts have been shipping in reinforcements. Not just their own but mercenary groups, too."

"But where to?" asked a Corporal from transport. "How could they conceal them in the Complex?"

"They didn't." Kuruk moved up to stand by me at the head of the table in the canteen we were using.

"It has been verified that the Sparts have been shipping in heavy plant. Earth moving equipment, mostly. In order to do so, they have constructed one or more air bases nearby. That is where they have been landing their reinforcements. That is the intel I have received."

Kuruk withdrew a folded sheet of paper from inside his smock and carefully unfolded it. He touched it softly, smoothing out the creases. It was a map, heavily bloodstained.

"This came from... from a brave man we had working on the inside. I was to deliver this to the CO on arrival at the Hub."

The group crowded around for a closer look. It was a crude map but had enough detail to show the location of two bases, one to the north and one to the south of the Hub.

The corporal waved his hands."How the fuck can they build something like this and we not know about it? What the fuck are the Navy doing upstairs?"

Slade made as if to answer but I cut in.

"That's not important right now. What we have to do is decide on our next course of action. Do we hold here and wait for communication, or do we head up to the Hub or down to the Complex? Sounds like both would be grateful for fresh troops."

Chatter started immediately, soon growing to a shouting match. I guess everyone had been rattled by the chopper attack. But I needed to restore order so I put two pistol shots into the ceiling. Having got everyone's attention, I outlined a few ideas and suggested we sleep on it and make a decision in the morning. I left Pops to organise the night stags and went in search of a drink. God knows, I needed one.

CHAPTER 20

THE HIGHWAY

I was up before dawn and the news coming in wasn't good. Still nothing from the Complex end and only a brief message from the Hub reporting that the area was under sustained attack. There were no new orders coming through so I figured it was up to us to decide on a course of action.

Following a breakfast conflab, the decision was taken to keep a small holding force here at the Station, while the rest of us struck up the Highway towards the Hub. We would take the wounded with us, loading them into the few vehicles we had that were still operational. Within a couple of hours the group was ready to go. Leaving about thirty personnel behind, we had a group of eight GTVs, two APCs, twenty support staff and around forty combat troops, plus our team. Most were armed but ammo was in short supply.

The sky was clear again, though Pops pointed out the heavy clouds on the horizon. More reason to move. If we stayed put, we may well get snowed in. Though, on the plus side, bad weather would ground the Sparts too. I took up position in the lead APC and distributed the team amongst the rest of the convoy. We put a few spotters up on the outside of some of the vehicles to watch out for any air activity. They had to switch around often, though; the temperature was below zero when stationary, let alone any wind chill.

Some bods had been out first thing and cleared away what wreckage they could from the Highway. The rest we would just have to deal with as we came upon it. There was plenty of it, too. It was slow going picking our way through the debris. We used the APCs to push wrecks aside here and there and I had one eye on those snow clouds moving in. We were about ten klicks out from the Hub when one of the spotters waved to me. I called a halt and ran over to his truck.

"Up there," he pointed, handing me his binos. "One of those copters."

I scanned the sky up ahead and, sure enough, there he was, circling at about fifty metres. I called the NCO's in for a quick chat. We decided to space out the convoy, sending the APCs on ahead. I'd have given anything for some decent AA cover but all we had were sidearms and one or two gimpys. Decision made, we pushed on.

To our advantage the sky began clouding over, the wind picked up, then light snow began to fall. The first trouble came about five klicks later. That well known whistle, followed by shells raining down, about twenty metres off to the south of the road. We got the GTVs off the road before the shells could zero in. There was no cover around, so I got the troops to dismount and take position further out to the sides. I decided to push on ahead with the APCs; they could move fast and had some protection. The light was beginning to fade and I wanted to see what was in front of us.

The growing gloom worked in our favour. The road ahead lay like a flat, grey ribbon rolled out across the snowy plain. Our APCs, camo painted as they were and with running lights switched off, had some measure of concealment. Not so the forces laid out ahead. I called for the driver to stop and both vehicles pulled up. Using the binos from the top hatch, I saw a large group of twinkling lights ahead.

In the hazy distance, I could just make out the perimeter of the Hub. Tracer fire travelled in both directions over and through it. I could see burning buildings behind the wire and plumes of smoke lifting into the air. Between us and the camp lay the Spart forces, dozens of APCs and other armoured vehicles, with infantry gathered around them. Closest to us sat a line of self propelled artillery, the guns that had been firing earlier, I guess. I scanned back to the perimeter and spotted where, in places, the Sparts looked to be breaking through.

As I watched, a transport took off from inside the Hub. It immediately attracted ground fire from the Spart forces. For a minute, I thought the transport would escape, but a missile clipped the back end of it and the ship hovered for a moment then lurched and flipped sideways, crashing back down to the ground.

A closer movement caught my eye. Three APCs and a truck heading our way. A recce group, no doubt, come to see what was left after the bombardment. I immediately dropped back down into the vehicle and ordered the driver to hightail it back to the convoy. There wasn't much time so I swiftly placed troops in ambush position ahead of the group. We set a gimpy up each side of the Highway, quickly digging positions in the snow. Devlin disappeared off into the gloom with his sniper rifle, the rest of us checked magazines and waited.

Minutes later, the first enemy APC came into view. It halted, I could hear the engine ticking over. The top hatch popped open and a head appeared, lifting a pair of binos. Before they reached his eyes there was a spray of red followed by the echo of a shot. I grinned. Devlin was on form, as usual. At my command, the gimpys opened up, lazy lines of tracer arcing out to hit the tarmac then working their way up to the APC, pinging off the sides. There was little chance of causing damage but I was playing for time.

The driver, no doubt unnerved by the corpse falling back into his vehicle plus the gimpy fire, immediately shot into reverse and disappeared back up the Highway. Round one to us. I kept the teams in place for the moment and doubled back to the main group. As night was drawing in, we made the decision to drop back, hopefully out of artillery range and laager up. Because of the snow we couldn't move too far off the Highway but we got the GTVs into a defensive position and settled in for the night.

The worst thing was the cold. As darkness fell the snow became heavier and, within an hour it was a full on blizzard. All the vehicles had built-in heaters but it meant keeping engines running all night. Fuel wasn't too much of an issue, it wasn't as though we had a long drive, forward or back, but it grated to be using resources while standing still.

Dawn came, frosty and bright. We dug the trucks out and made ready to move again. As the way ahead was blocked, we decided to fall back to the Station. We at least had cover and supplies there.

The clearer weather meant we travelled fast but it also brought the choppers out again. Our spotters saw them, four of the bastards, coming in fast and low to our left. There's a natural tendency to bunch together when under attack but that was the worst thing to do in this situation. Given our lack of decent AA fire, we had every vehicle space out and put their foot down. We had the gimpys mounted on the APCs; one at the front, one at the back of the column. They opened fire even before the choppers came into range, hoping to put the pilots off, perhaps. There was little else we could do. We were lined up like ducks in a row, standing out against the snowy white background. The choppers swept in, machine guns blazing, pinpricks of light flashing, followed by the whine of bullets, the crash of a truck overturning.

Javez at the gimpy on the lead APC had a good eye, though. Judging the time and distance perfectly, she sent out a stream of tracer that the lead chopper flew directly through. Pieces flew off the machine, followed by thick white smoke from its engine. The chopper pulled its nose up sharply, the pilot must have been hit. It climbed up, flipped over, and crashed down with a dull thud into the snow. Seconds later, it exploded in an orange ball of flame.

If the other choppers were discouraged, they didn't show it. However the convoy was putting up a mass of small arms fire now which at least kept the buggers at some distance. With a last attacking run, they turned and disappeared off into the distance. Pausing only to pick up wounded, we sped on southwards, reaching the Station with no further incident. We left behind three GTVs and sixteen dead - and all for nothing, I thought.

There was better news at the Station. Some units had made their way up from the front lines, including a heavy machine gun troop which would give us some decent AA cover. They had been through it, though. A major Spart attack had come out of the Complex, overseen by more of those choppers. Much of our line had been overrun though forces were still holding out in parts of the trench line. There were even some still holding out in the Complex itself. However, we could rely on no help from that area, nor would it make much sense to travel down there. For the moment we decided to stay put, the new arrivals strengthening our defensive position.

Doc had taken charge of the wounded. I popped into the med building to see how she was doing. She looked haggard. I imagine she had been up all night tending to the casualties. She gave me a sitrep, it was grim. The med station here was not equipped for major incidents, it was more of a halfway house. I thanked her and sent her off to get some rest. Just then Pops wandered in and asked me to join him.

I followed him back over to the canteen, where a group of NCOs and a couple of officers had gathered. Immediate defensive plans had been put into operation but we still had the question of what to do in the longer term. Each spoke their piece, the new arrivals filling us in on the Spart attack out of the Complex. Pops ran them through our excursion up the Highway. It was clear that, even with the new arrivals we didn't have enough numbers to break through the Spart forces surrounding the Hub. Even if we did, it was doubtful anything was taking off.

Our second option was to move east to reinforce the positions still holding at the Complex. Perhaps we could make a difference there but, as we had seen, any movement along the Highway would likely come under air attack.

There had been no contact with upstairs, so we had no indication of whether reinforcements would be descending from above. In light of all that everyone agreed that the sensible option was to firm up here, at least for now. We had supplies, shelter and could dig in to await developments. That decided, I set off to grab some scoff and get my head down for a couple of hours. Before I got too far, though, Kuruk appeared at my elbow.

"Skip, there is another option, you know?" he murmured.

"Go on." I prompted, banging the gedunk machine when my cheese roll refused to drop into the chute. My SDC didn't work so well on this model.

"We cut across to one of the new Spart bases, hijack a transport and get back upstairs."

"Wow." I gave the machine another thump and smirked as my scran finally appeared. "Just a short hike across a snow covered plain, avoiding any Spart patrols, then waltz into their base and fly off, just like that?"

Kuruk's face fell and I realised what an arse I was being. I grabbed my roll. "Sorry, Kuruk, I've had about three hours sleep this last few days. I presume you have a plan in mind."

He did, him and Pops had been talking it through. Thing is, we had some important intel to get back upstairs. It wasn't just a map that Kuruk's brother had brought out, there was an E-stick containing all the data he'd managed to download from the Spart command mainframe, too. I agreed provisionally but really needed to get my head down before making a final decision. We scheduled a meeting for later that afternoon.

Come dusk, suitably refreshed - I'd even managed to grab lukewarm shower - I called the team together in Webb's old office. Someone had been busy while I was catching up on my beauty sleep. Kuruk had been comparing his brother's map to local survey ones and pinpointed the new Spart base locations. Armstrong and Koenig had been sniffing round all the buildings and had uncovered some winter survival gear and extra ammo and explosives. Doc had listed all the wounded and whether they could be moved or not. Javez and Slade had been working on coms and also tried hacking the Spart net. They'd even got a brief response from Abomo upstairs so we knew we had not yet been abandoned.

From the Sparts we learnt that more forces were being fed in via the two new bases, including armour. Pops figured it would be a bonus if we could inflict some damage if and when we reached a base.

Vitali and Khan had been on a scout round of our defensive positions, just to ensure everything was ship-shape. So far, there had been no sign of Spart forces from north or south. Cloud had been low all day with intermittent snow so that, at least, had kept the choppers grounded. McNulty and Weaver had collected what weapons they could for the team. Half our stuff had gone up in the APC but they cobbled together a reasonable amount of sidearms and ammo for us. We would be travelling light and fast in any case.

Referring to the map, Kuruk indicated the base to the east.

"This is the main and nearest Spart base," he motioned. "But, f course, this one lies on the other side of the Rift. So getting to it would mean travelling through the Complex. Not an easy task, especially if we are talking about bringing the wounded with us."

Slade continued the briefing. "The plain sweeps away on both directions. Here you see it is cut by this large river. The base to the north is built in a slight rise on the river bank. The plain is largely open but there is a large forested area just to the west of the base which may provide some cover on the final approach."

"So that's what, a distance of fifty, sixty klicks out in the snow? On foot, I presume, as the snow will be too deep for GTVs. At what, ten klicks a day? That's around a week, providing the weather doesn't worsen."

Slade nodded, looking chastened but Vitali grinned. "When do we start?"

Pops spoke up. "If we plan to take the wounded we can transport them in the APCs. Doc tells me that those who can be moved will just about fit in them."

"We are set on taking the wounded?" asked Weaver.

"Yes," I responded. "The troops here aren't saying it, and I'm not mentioning it either, but if the Sparts come up or down the road in force, the Station can't hold out for long. Given that, I wouldn't want our wounded falling into their hands, especially after some of the stories I've heard from the Rubble Rats."

The group murmured in agreement.

"Besides," added Pops, "if they are in the APCs, they won't slow us down. There are no roads out there so it's cross country and, given the depth of the snow, the APCs won't be running at full speed."   He nodded to Koenig who stepped forward.

"Amongst other things Armstrong and I found some winter shelters in the stores. Should be enough to see us through a week's travel."

I nodded in approval. "Good. Any objections then?" None came. We all knew the risks; the weather could change, navigation could be a problem, we might run into Spart forces. But I knew my people, they would rather be active than sit around waiting for something to happen.

We ran through final details, then set a start time for midnight. I told everyone to grab some rest before leaving. Before that, though, we held a small gathering to say goodbye to our departed friend.

I was shaken awake even earlier than I'd planned by Pops.

"You better come and see this!" he said as I swore at him. Rubbing my eyes, I jacketed up and followed him over to the canteen.

"There's another group just arrived from the Complex," Pops told me. "Led by Gage."

"Shit!" I muttered as we entered the building. Gage had wasted no time in taking over. He held rank above everyone else here and had called together the NCOs. He was well into one of his motivational speeches when Pops and I entered.

"Go and make sure the rest are ready to leave soon, will you?" I murmured to Pops. "Tell Doc to prepare the wounded." Pops nodded and left, I turned back to Gage. Surrounded by a group of bored and irritated faces, he was now outlining his plan for a counter-thrust south to rout the rebel forces.

"But sir," one NCO objected. "We have limited ammo supplies and would be cut to pieces on any approach by the Spart air cover. Here at least we have -"

Gage cut him short with a wave. "I understand if you have no stomach for a fight, corporal, but your job here is clear!"

The corporal swore under his breath and stepped back. Then Gage caught sight of me.

"Ah, Naylor, excellent. Your team will make a welcome addition to our strike force!"

I moved to face Gage.

"My team are moving out within the hour, with anyone who wants to join us. We are striking north towards the new Spart base, from where we will attempt to get off this frozen rock and back upstairs to the loving arms of the Navy. The wounded who can be moved are coming with us. As for the rest, I advise you listen to the corporal here, he is talking sense. Dig in and wait for reinforcements, that's my advice."

Gage bristled. "You forget who is senior rank here, Naylor!"

I stepped in close to him and hissed in his face.

"And you forget what I said to you on our first meeting. You've cost me two good men already and it is only the fact that I want to maintain morale and discipline for the rest of the troops here that I haven't knocked you on your arse already!"

Gage coughed and reddened, then stepped back. "Well, yes, perhaps you are right. The corporal has a good point. Very well, we will make firm our position here. Meanwhile, I will accompany Naylor and his team in order to carry news of the situation to HQ."

Oh God, I thought, that's all I needed. Still, I could at least keep an eye in the idiot if he was with us. Or maybe just leave him out on the steppe...

CHAPTER 21

THE STEPPE

Just over an hour later, the departees were gathered around the two remaining APCs. The wounded were on board and the survival gear stowed on top of each vehicle. The team were all loaded up with whatever weapons and ammo they could carry. Everyone was wrapped in blankets and greatcoats over their snow gear. About fifteen other troops had decided to join us, along with Gage, skulking at the back. Kuruk was looking daggers at him. I pulled aside one of the new-comers, I recognised him as one of Yao's squad.

"Any news on Yao?" I asked.

The trooper shook his head.

"Our squad was split up in the last attack. Last time

I saw her, she was heading up the trench line with a squad. Not long after that we were pushed back. We re-grouped behind the lines,then evacced to here. It's a real mess down there."

Seeing my expression he slapped me on the shoulder. "Don't worry. The Boss is a survivor. She'll make it out."

There was a blast on a whistle to round everyone up and get us in marching order. A small group led off to scout ahead, the rest of us formed up around the APCs. On the way out I saw the corporal from earlier. He saluted and shook my hand.

"Good luck, sir. Don't forget to remind the brass upstairs we're still here."

I clapped him on the shoulder. "Don't worry, I'll tell them. I'll get someone down here as quick as. You'll be chugging on Navy rum before you know it."

We set off across the Highway and into the dark. Javez had rigged up a couple of compasses. The EMF played havoc with normal equipment but she had come up with a gadget that should give us at least a semi-accurate reading, backed up by marking the position of sunset and sunrise each day. We aimed to travel mostly at night, there was precious little cover out on the plains during daylight hours.

Within minutes, we were in darkness. The only light was the pale glow of the snow reflecting the moon's weak rays. A light snow was falling. Good, that would cover our tracks. I kept the recce team close in, only a short way ahead. I figured there would likely be little Spart patrolling activity in these conditions.

A couple of hours out and the recce crew reported back to say they'd found a sheltered area ahead, a slight dip in the plain. It made sense to stop there, parking the APCs as a wind break and getting the survival shelters set up. Each shelter came with its own heater but I ordered everyone to be careful with running them, keeping a low constant heat rather than turning them up high then back down, in order to conserve fuel. A couple of the team had thoughtfully brought white bed sheets that we draped around the vehicles to break up the outline of the APCs. After sorting out a stag rota, we all settled in for shuteye.

I stayed up a little longer, doing one last round to double check everything. So it was that I saw the dawn break over the snowy plain. The lightening sky was suddenly filled with a pink glow that spread out and across the whiteness below. The frost glittered and a flight of birds swept across my view in a perfect V formation, the first wildlife I'd seen since arriving. There was a cold, majestic beauty to the whole scene and for the first time on this frozen rock, I relaxed. Whatever lay ahead, we were at least now in charge of our own destiny.

I woke at around 1300, Khan pushing a mug of hot coffee towards me. It had started snowing again. Not heavily, but enough we hoped to keep the Spart choppers grounded. Javez had made her calculations and was talking to the recce ream. I checked with Doc to see how the wounded were doing. She reported no problems so far, though she'd had to turf Gage out of one of the APCs. He apparently thought it should be his personal command vehicle. I shook my head in disbelief. Then we were off into the snow again, the APCs on their broad tracks skimming slowly across the surface, the rest of us wading knee deep.

Still, we made good going. Just a couple of rest pauses, before we struck camp again before dawn. Not such a nice view this time. The cloud had settled in and the snowfall was heavier. It got worse as the day went on, by noon it was a full blizzard. We decided to press on anyway, as there would be even less chance of being spotted.

I recalled the recce team and told everyone to work in groups of six. Each person was to keep a hand on the shoulder of the person in front. Squad leaders were to follow close behind the last person of the squad before them. The APCs were positioned front and back, the squads formed in lines between them.

From then on it was down to slogging, step by step,

through the driving snow. Hoods up, faces wrapped in mufflers against the bitter cold, we snaked pace by pace across that seemingly endless plain. There was no concept of time passing, just the numbing cold, the back of the person in front of you and the feeling of a hand on your shoulder. All eyes were turned down, trying to find shelter from the driving snow that stung the face like a hundred ice needles. The world became a very small place indeed, just a patch of snow and a dirty snowsuit ahead.

By evening the blizzard had worsened and we were reduced to a stumbling, staggering mess. Progress was painfully slow and there was a real chance of individuals being separated and lost. We decided to pitch camp and sit out the rest of the storm. Doc did the rounds, ensuring that everyone removed socks and boots inside the shelters and dried them over the heaters. Not the most pleasant sight or smell but frostbite out here was a virtual death sentence.

The storm laid in for most of the day and night. It wasn't until midnight that it died off. Once it had, we set off again, the clear sky giving us some welcome moonlight to navigate by. To make up time, we decided to press on into the next morning. The sunlight, weak as it was, did something to lift spirits. It was about an hour after dawn when the cry came up from McNulty at his watch station on the lead APC.

"Chopper!" he indicated up away to the north.

The column halted immediately, all of us dropping into the snow. The chopper glinted as the morning sun sparkled off its windscreen and the faint thrum of rotor blades reached us across the frozen air. I swear we all held our breath as the machine continued on, it looked like he hadn't spotted us. A minute later and the sound faded into the distance. Brushing ourselves down, we stood and made off again.

The clear weather didn't last, those mountainous clouds on the horizon swept quickly in and the snow began to fall lightly. Early afternoon, we stopped for a rest break as the snowfall grew more dense, visibility soon dropping down to a few metres. I was having a syg with Vitali, trying to get some shelter at the side of one the APCs when he clutched my arm and dropped his syg in the snow. Then I heard it, too. A hissing sound. Seconds later, shapes loomed out of the gloom, sweeping past us at speed. Ski troops! Had they seen us?

The word was quickly and quietly passed along the line, weapons were readied, defensive positions taken. The only sound was the whisper of the cold wind. Then it came again, that hiss, followed by the crackle of small arms fire.

The team responded immediately. McNulty swung

the gimpy in a wide arc, shooting violet tracer out into the murk. Bullets whipped back around us. Vitali, kneeling next to me, hummed "The bullets fly and lift us to Heaven," before raising his pistol and taking pot shots at the vague shapes that swept past. A dark, round object flew through the air.

"Grenade!" I shouted and dropped. With a dull crump and tongue of orange flame, it exploded nearby. Fortunately, the snow muffled the effect, but still shrapnel sizzled as it flew past, one piece catching me on the cheek.

As quickly as they came, the ski troops vanished. We held positions for a few more minutes, then I quickly rounded everyone up. Three of the Station troops had been wounded, one seriously. Doc came over to fuss at my face, I was okay, the fragment had torn through my head scarf and given me a cut but that was it. She handed me a medstrip then turned back to supervise getting the newly wounded into an APC. That done, we set back off at once. We needed to change position fast, the weather might clear at any moment and that ski squad may be able to call in air support.

I pushed the group hard for the next several hours. The weather stayed the same, sparing any visits from above. Luckily we saw no more ski troops either. I gave the team a quick rest around midnight, before pushing on again until just before dawn. Everyone was starting to flag now. A few were reporting stabbing pains in the eyes.

"Snow blindness," explained Vitali. We had no goggles but Schrader doled out his supply of aviator shades, which brought some relief. Thanks to Doc's advice, we had no cases of frostbite. However, it was clear we couldn't last much longer out here. We were down to a few hours fuel in the heaters and some of the wounded were in a bad way. We had lost one already, the soldier wounded in the ski attack. Doc broke off his tags and we fashioned a makeshift mound in the snow, the best we could do in the circumstances.

I had a conflab with the team and we decided that while the group would firm up where we were for the day, a recce group would push ahead to see how close we were to our destination. Khan, Pops, Weaver and Armstrong chewed down a last jerky stick then set off into the rose-tinted plain. We did what we could to keep the wounded comfortable, then settled in, huddled together in the shelters, sharing out the last of the rations.

The recce team returned late afternoon. It was good news. The forest adjacent to the Spart base lay directly ahead. I gave the team the food that we had saved for them, let them grab an hour's rest, then we set out on what we hoped was the last leg of the journey.

Sure enough, a couple of hours later we could make out a dark smudge on the horizon. Not long after we were in the lee of the forest, glad to be out of the biting wind. I didn't want to risk going through the forest at night, the darkness inside looked complete. We pitched camp on the very edge, I even allowed the gathering of firewood to build a couple of fires under cover of the trees. I figured that keeping warm was more important than the risk of being spotted though, on Williams' suggestion, I had some of the group use branches to sweep away our tracks in the snow.

Pops woke me up before dawn, pushing a mug towards me. "The last of the coffee." he said with a grin. "Come and have a look at this."

I followed him out of the tent and along the tree line. As we went on, he slowed down and bade me crouch, then drop into a crawl. Vitali and Devlin were laid prone ahead, behind the cover of a fallen tree.

"Look!" Devlin motioned ahead. I poked my head slowly over the log to see an impressive sight.   A group of around half a dozen animals stood just outside the edge of the forest. They were like Earth wolves but much larger. Stood motionless, breath clouding in the dawn air, grey eyes bright as they surveyed the plain ahead. At some unspoken signal one padded off into the trees, to return followed by, what I guess, was the rest of the pack including young cubs. We watched spellbound, suddenly oblivious to the cold, as the pack made their way out of the trees and padded away from us along the tree line, disappearing from view.

Soon, only one remained, a big old male. I swear he looked directly at our position, briefly pulling lips back over large, yellowing canines. Then, with a shake of his shaggy head, he turned and was also gone.

We all let out a breath and returned, wordless, to camp where we found the group ready to move. Slade and Weaver had already carried out a quick recce into the trees and the news was mixed. On the plus side, we wouldn't be wading through snow and there was no wind chill. On the minus side, it would be difficult going for the APCs. The forest was dense in places and the closer we got to the base, the quieter we needed to move. We made the decision to take the APCs in as far as we could, then play things by ear.

After days of blank whiteness, the sight of green, living things and seeing shade and colour raised spirits somewhat and, I don't know why, I took the sight of the wolf pack as a good omen.

We got about an hour in before having to abandon the APCs. We had a few stretchers and improvised some more from branches for the non-walking wounded. The rest had to stumble along the best they could, supported by a fellow trooper. I put Pops, Vitali and Devlin out on point and it was as we were having a rest break later that afternoon that they reported back.

"There's a road ahead." Vitali told us. He asked Kuruk for his map. Kuruk unfolded it and passed it over. Pops shone a torch so we could all see.

"Yes, here," Vitali ran a finger along the line on the map.

"It's not much more than a track," observed Pops, "but it looks well maintained and is clear of snow."

Kuruk explained. "The base is on the site of an old geological survey outpost. I imagine they were set up when this planet was first scouted for minerals. I'm guessing that track heads through the forest, then over to the Hub. It must be the main route the Sparts are using to transport their forces across there."

"Okay," I responded. "Let's get the whole group moved up and keep eyes on. If nothing else, it gives us a direct route to the base. Otherwise we could be wandering around out here for days."

Weapons readied and with the recce team leading, we moved the group up close to the track. In the darkening gloom it appeared as a light ribbon, cutting an almost straight path through the tall, narrow trees. The evening was silent apart from a whisper of breeze through the branches.   Devlin moved up onto the road and peered left and right, then signalled to the rest of us. If anyone had been watching we must have looked like ghosts; white figures materialising noiselessly out of the dark forest. We established a marching order, two lines on each side of the track with a point and rearguard, then began moving slowly east.

CHAPTER 22

THE TRACK

We had been going for around forty minutes when Devlin sprinted up to me near the head of the column.

"Engine noises, approaching from the west," he growled. We immediately waved everyone off the track, putting the wounded deeper into the forest. By now the sound of engines was audible to all and soon a flash of lights could be seen in the distance. I had a quick chat with the team and outlined a plan. We sat Vitali at the edge of the track, bandaged shoulder clearly visible, Doc stood over him, med kit open and pretending to attend to him. The rest of us were placed out of sight along the track.

The engine sound grew louder, trucks from the sound

of it, plus a smaller vehicle. Then they were going by us, a quad bike with wrapped up rider, followed by three trucks. They were of a type I'd not seen before, the cabs were wheeled like a regular truck but the bodies sat on tracks. The gears gunned down as the convoy slowed.

Doc played her part well, moving to the centre of the track and waving a torch, bringing the vehicles to a halt. We had removed hers and Vitali's camo gear and weapons, giving Doc a thermal blanket to wrap herself in. The quad bike rider halted and dismounted, the trucks behind also stopping, engines ticking over. With a nudge, I signalled Weaver and he and Armstrong ran in a low crouch to the rearmost truck. Along the line the rest of the team were moving towards the other vehicles. Vitali, meanwhile, had stood up and, dropping a pistol from inside his bandage to his hand, put two bullets into the bike rider.

Within seconds, the truck drivers had been pulled from their cabs and lined up, hands on heads at the roadside, faces pale in the torchlight. The rider's body had already been moved off into the trees as the trucks were searched.

"What's the haul?" I asked Slade.

"Three trucks, three drivers. One truck is empty, apart from some old boxes and crates. Truck two has some kit and supplies, truck three also empty. According to one of the drivers they have just delivered supplies and ammo to the front line at the Hub."

"Do they have any papers? Ask them about security at the base."

A few minutes later and Slade returned. The drivers, taken completely by surprise, offered little resistance to questioning.

"No papers. Security is quite lax, from the sound of it. They seem to think they are safe here, far away from the fighting."

Pops chuckled. "Thank Heaven for amateurs."

I nodded in agreement, the beginnings of a plan forming in my mind.

"Secure the prisoners. Put out a point front, bring everyone back up on the road"

I smiled at Doc as she came over.

"Good work, Doc. You missed your vocation."

She laughed. "Can I suggest we load our wounded onto the trucks for now? If nothing else it will keep them off the ground and out of the cold."

"Yep, good idea. Break out the last of the rations for them too. Hopefully, by tomorrow we will be out of here."

She nodded and turned away. Kuruk came over, pointing to his map.

"I had a chat with one of the drivers. I think we are here, which puts us only about three klicks from the base. I was thinking we might use these trucks to get in."

I grinned. "Trojan trucks. Great minds think alike. Call everyone over except the point. Let's run through some ideas".

Dawn found us further along the track, approaching the base. Our wounded were in the rears trucks. Devlin had scooted ahead on the quad bike, muffled up, sniper rifle slung across his back. We slowed and stopped as he came back along the track towards us. I got out and walked over to him. Removing his goggles, he clapped his hands together and stood, stretching his back.

"The road curves ahead then drops down into a dip. From there, it leaves the forest and then it's about half a klick to the base entrance."

"Security?"

"A wire fence around most of the perimeter. Entrance post is a standard kiosk and pole, two guards in the box. They've been busy, though. Looks like three field runways and an assortment of prefabs and hangars. Couldn't get too close but I clocked two transports at the end of the runways."

"Okay, here's what we'll do. Move the column up to the curve and settle in for the moment. Then we'll send a recce team in to have a good look around. There's no point charging in blind. We need to know exactly where everything is, especially those transports."

Devlin nodded and I sent him off to sit in the truck to warm up. Taking the quad, I led the group up to the curve in the road and had them park the trucks along the edge, in as much cover as we could get from the trees. Then, calling everyone together, I explained the plan.

"Heads up, listen in. A recce team goes in while there is still light to bring back detailed info on the layout of the place. Once we have that, then, just before dawn, we take the trucks in. Truck drivers will be wearing Spart jackets. Assuming we get in with no problem, we head for a transport, then up and away. Questions?"

"Any sign of choppers?" asked Slade. "Could make life difficult if they get airborne before we do."

Devlin leaned in. "I didn't see any in the open but there are some hangars there, so we can probably assume there are choppers."

Schrader interjected. "If they are hangered, it shouldn't be an issue. I'll need a couple of minutes to get a transport off the ground. It should take them longer than that to scramble the choppers in these conditions. If we lift before they do, we can point up and outrun them easily. If they are up before us, well, we'd be a sitting duck."

"Okay, so we need to get straight in and onto a transport." I said.

That decided, I put together a recce team of three, led by Vitali. Gage surprised everyone by volunteering to go, too. He had been quiet up to now, almost invisible. I shrugged and nodded, perhaps he felt left out.

Once kitted out, the four man recce team disappeared into the trees, planning to cut through the forest until they reached its edge at a point where they could overlook the base. I told everyone else to rest up until they returned.

As it turned out, they didn't return. At least not all of them. Only one came back, one of the regular troopers, running down the track. He passed the point man and we jumped out of the trucks as he ran up. Panting, he gasped, "Captured! They've been captured!"

We got the lad calmed down and he told us what had happened. The team had made it to the edge of the forest, then crawled across some open ground, taking cover in a dip from which they had a good view over the whole base. As they settled in to begin obs, a Spart patrol was making its way along the perimeter of the base. The patrol would've passed about fifty metres from the our team but concealment was good, so all they had to do was lay low.

Gage had other ideas, though. According to the lad, as the patrol approached, Gage stood and raised his arms, shouting to them "We surrender!"

The rest of the team tried to pull him back down into cover but too late, they had been spotted. Gage broke free and stumbled towards the Sparts. Within seconds the patrol reached them and an APC shot out from the base towards them.

"I asked Vitali should we fight?" the lad said. "But it was clear we were outnumbered and we had no cover and nowhere to go. Gage was already at the patrol, they were fanning out, weapons raised. Vitali whispered to me to make a break for it, he would create a diversion. As the patrol got closer he threw down his gun but then launched himself at them. I ran for the trees, some shots whizzed over my head but I made it into cover. I'm sorry, sir, should I have stayed?"

"No lad," I clapped him on the shoulder, "You did the right thing. Shit, this changes things."

I sent the soldier off and called the team round again, explaining the situation.

"We need to go in now, before our guys are questioned. Vitali will hold out but who knows what Gage will tell them?"

"What if he's talked already?" asked Slade.

"We have to take that chance. The longer we delay, the worse our odds."

"And our guys?" asked Khan.

"There's no way we're leaving without Vitali and the

other two but how to get to them?" I wondered. It was Javez who came up with the solution.

"The chips! The implants, we can use those to track him. Give me five minutes, let me see what I can rig up."

"The atmospherics?" I enquired.

"Could be a problem but we are further from the mine here. Besides, we don't need to be super accurate, if we can determine which building he is in, that will do. I'll get right on it, Skip."

"Good. Right, we keep the wounded in two trucks. They go in first and head straight for the closest transport. I'll take the other truck and go for Vitali and the others and get them to the transport. Devlin, you head out before us on the quad, see if you can find a position on the perimeter to cover us on the way in, then get down to the transport quick as you can."

Devlin nodded, pulled his wrap back round his face and jumped back onto the quad, gunning the engine and shooting off into the twilight. Meanwhile, the trucks were being loaded. I noticed the Spart prisoners, hands zip-tied, stood off to the side. I walked over, waving for Doc and Pops to join me.

"You and you," I pointed to two of them. "Get your jackets off. Pops, release their hands, then re-tag and gag them and put them in the second truck."

Pops nodded and cut the ties so the two men could

remove their khaki padded jackets. The third driver, an older guy, looked uneasy as I moved to him, taking out my knife. He was relieved when I cut his ties too.

"You are going to drive the first truck. It's better that the guards see a familiar face. Oh and Pops here will be right next to you in the cab. One wrong move and he will kill you. Understand?"

The driver nodded repeatedly. I turned to Pops.

"Put on one of those jackets, Pops. Doc, the other jacket is for you. I want you in the back of the first truck. Put the worst looking wounded closest to the entrance. If the guards take a look I want them to see badly wounded friends, clear? Hide anything that might give us away."

Doc nodded and moved to the truck. Pops had the Spart jacket on and, grabbing the driver by the arm, escorted him to the cab. I motioned our other two prisoners towards the second truck. Armstrong and Khan were stood by it.

"Get these two in the back, up by the cab. Khan, stay with and keep eyes on. Either of them makes a noise, you kill them both. Got it?" Khan nodded and began hoisting the men into the rear of the truck.

"Armstrong, you drive the second truck. Schrader, you're in the cab with him. Anything goes wrong, head straight for the transport and get off, don't wait for the rest of us."

"But Skip - " Schrader began. I cut him short.

"Don't wait! Your priority is to get Kuruk and the wounded off as quick as. Is that clear?"

"Crystal, Skip" Schrader nodded. I motioned for Kuruk and Slade to get in the second truck. McNulty, Williams and Weaver climbed in the back of the third truck, I jumped into driver's seat. Javez jumped in alongside me, fiddling with some device in her hands. With everyone aboard I sounded the horn, signalling the lead truck to move out. I flicked my syg out of the window and we rolled off into the lengthening shadows.

CHAPTER 23

THE BASE

We kept the pace steady and, within a few minutes, rounded the curve in the track and saw it run down to the base. There wasn't much to see in the twilight gloom, just a couple of lights twinkling at the guard post. We rumbled slowly down to the barrier and came to a stop, engines chugging and smoking in the cold air. Two sentries came out of the kiosk. One stood by, weapon slung ready, while the other jumped on the running board to speak to the lead driver. Some words were exchanged, then the sentry moved round to the back of the truck and pulled back the flap. Even from where I was, I could hear Doc's stern voice.

"Shut that flap, we have wounded in here!"

In spite of the tenseness of the situation I had to smile. Seconds later, the sentry moved back towards the barrier and waved us on. Keeping things nice and calm, looking straight ahead, we drove slowly in as the barrier lifted. So far, so good! The two leading trucks peeled off to the right.

"Javez, speak to me." I murmured out the side of my mouth.

She swore and banged the device against the dash. In the dark cab, it gave off a pale green glow. Then she pointed ahead.

"There, those buildings. I'm getting a weak signal but it has to be them."

I nodded and steered along the rough track towards a collection of squat portacabins.

Javez fiddled with the controls some more.

"That one, there."

I pulled up and stopped outside the end cabin, then muttered to the crew in the back.

"Ready? We go in fast and hard, try and keep noise to a minimum. Anyone gets separated, get over to the transport as best you can. Okay, here we go."

I slipped the truck into neutral, pulled up the handbrake and opened the door. Sliding out of the seat, I brought my AK up to the ready and cocked it. We moved quietly and quickly to the door. On a three count, I kicked it in and moved inside, sweeping the gun across the space. First room, empty. One door and a corridor.

I motioned McNulty and Weaver to go for the door, the rest with me to the corridor. As I did, a figure appeared, cup in hand, puzzled look on his face. Before he could react, I hit him with the butt of my gun and he dropped heavily to the floor. I was already into the corridor, Javez tight on my shoulder.

"Shit, I've lost the signal." she said.

There was shot from behind us and, in response, a door at the end of our corridor opened. A figure came out, reaching to its holster. I gave a short burst from the hip and the Spart was flung back into the room. I headed straight on, Javez covering my six from the other two doors in the corridor.

Bursting into the room, I saw three hooded figures tied to chairs. A man stood behind one of them, pistol pointed to a seated figure's head. From the bloodstained dressing, I guessed it was Vitali. The man with the gun made to speak. Before he could, I swept up the AK and gave him a single shot. He crashed to the floor, his face a red ruin. I wasn't in the mood to negotiate.   The rest of the room was empty, just some chairs and a table, on which lay some implements and a blood stained rag. I moved in and removed the hood of the first figure. Vitali squinted up at me, face battered and bloodied, one eye swollen shut.

"Well, you took your time," he said.

I slung my AK and began cutting his bonds.

"You okay?"

"I had worse beatings before. But they had moved onto other methods." He raised his good arm. Shit. Two fingers had been cut off his right hand. Vitali grinned at my expression.

"Guess I'll have to cancel those piano lessons."

I got him free and he stood shakily, so I moved to the other two figures. The second was a trooper, similarly battered. He was unconscious but I brought him round and got him free, too. That just left one figure, sat bolt upright and motionless in the chair. I whipped off the hood. Gage blinked back at me, looking terrified, with not a mark on him. I turned away to Vitali.

"What happened?"

Vitali shrugged and pointed to the trooper. "This guy - not a word, even when they beat him." He sneered and pointed to Gage. "This guy, first thing he tells them is that I am Spec Ops. That's why I got the extra treatment. Next, he tells them what an important man he is, who his Uncle is and how he would be a valuable prisoner. *Treat me right and I can give you lots of info*, is what he said."

He nudged the body in the floor with his toe.

"Luckily for us, our friend here was not high up enough in the pecking order to make a decision on that, so we were waiting for the arrival of some bigwig. Then you showed up."

I let out a sigh. "Okay. Help this guy out to the truck. Give me a minute and I'll be there. We're heading straight to the transport."

Supporting the groggy trooper, Vitali limped out of the room, leaving a small trail of bloodspots behind him. I turned to Gage. His eyes were filled with tears as he looked up at me. He had the look of a man who thinks he may be about to die. Turns out, he was right.

Jumping back into the cab, I revved the engine and we moved out towards the runway. It was then that the siren sounded. Fuck! I pressed down on the pedal, no point in stealth now. I could see lights going on and another sentry began running across the field towards us. He was about five metres away and raised his rifle directly at me. I was about to swerve right when the man's head vanished in a spray of blood and he fell. I smiled, good old Devlin!

Seconds later, we were at the rear of the transport, hurrying up the loading ramp. Devlin roared in on the quad, leapt off it and took up a firing position, rifle raised. I rushed through the passenger area, filled with the wounded and others, up to the flight deck. Schrader was frantically flicking switches and working the controls. Pops stood behind him.

"How long?" I asked urgently.

"Three minutes. I have to hack the security system then fire up the engines."

I glanced out of the windscreen. The siren was still going, lights were flickering on in the hangars and, as I watched, the doors of two of them were being slowly rolled open. There wasn't a lot of movement directly towards us, Devlin was doing a good job of keeping heads down. Schrader pointed over to the side.

"There's a problem. Over there, you see it? A heavy weapons emplacement, there's guys running to it. If they have AA or SAMs they'll shoot us out of the sky the minute we take off."

I nodded. "Alright, as soon as you can, take off, got it?" I clapped him on the shoulder and moved back to the loading ramp.

"Armstrong!" I shouted. "Pass me your grenades." Armstrong nodded and chucked me a bag of frag grenades. I slung it over my shoulder and changed the mag on my AK. I figured in the dark I could ride the quad over to the emplacement without too much risk of getting shot and do my best to neutralise the threat. After that? Well, who knew? Devlin was still crouched under the transport, sweeping the area in arcs. I squatted next to him.

"I'm heading over there. Give me covering fire for as long as you can, then get yourself on board and fuck off, clear?"

Devlin gave me a hard stare. "Clear, Skip." Then he looked up over my shoulder. Curious, I half turned, just as something walloped me in the face. Dazed, I hit the ground, feeling the bag of grenades being taken off me.

"Get him on board," I heard Pops voice say, as Devlin dragged me by my straps up the ramp. I struggled to my feet but Devlin had me in a tight grip.

"No!" I shouted to the figure of Pops as the ramp began to slowly close. He looked me in the eye, smiled and said, "Take care of them, Mike, they're a good bunch." Then he turned and disappeared into the darkness.

The engines began to whine. I turned and punched the bulkhead in frustration, then stormed up to the flight deck. Schrader, working feverishly, shouted over his shoulder, "Buckle up, this is going to be rough!"

The transport shuddered and began to lift. A line of violet tracer fire arced above us. Looking out the side screen I saw a series of explosions over at the emplacement and the tracer stopped. I also saw the hangar doors were now fully open, the choppers being towed out. Vehicles raced towards us, small arms fire pattered against the side of the ship.

"Here we go!" cried Schrader. He pulled hard on the controls and the transport lifted, then went nose up, almost vertical. Everyone tumbled around, things fell out of lockers, gear slid across the deck. I hoped that the worst of the wounded were secured. With a scream of protest the engines surged and propelled us skyward, the transport rattling and shaking like an old bus, our faces contorted as we pulled Gs. Within seconds the base was a small group of lights. A minute more and we were in total darkness. Schrader levelled out to a more conventional trajectory and let out a sharp breath. I could do nothing but sit stunned as we moved into the stratosphere.

The team were sat drinking coffee in a conference room on *Dolphin*. The transport had docked a few hours back and we'd all had a chance to shower and change into clean outfits. The wounded and other troops had all been separated and taken care of. We were being kept isolated until de-brief. Once up into space, we'd skimmed around the upper atmosphere until we managed to get a brief message through to a nearest Navy ship, which happened to be *Dolphin* and our old friend Captain Rahal. Things were a little tense for a while, we were in a Spart ship after all but, eventually, we were able to dock safe and sound.

For now, we were content to be clean and warm, although we were all feeling the loss of those we left behind, particularly Pops. The mood in the room was low. It's not as though we even got to complete our mission.

Slade and Schrader were both absent, the former was liasing with Navy Intel. The latter, well I had no idea where he was. Kuruk and his intel stayed close by me all the time, I wasn't about to let that info out of my sight after all the sacrifices made to get it. It was going to no one but Carswell. Call me jumpy but I was getting very particular about who I trusted with what.

We all looked up as Slade entered the room, accompanied by a Naval Officer. Slade introduced him as Barlow and explained he was to take the preliminary debrief sessions with us over the next day or so. In the meantime, we were to be confined to his particular area of the ship. SOP, I suppose, but irritating nonetheless. As far as Gage went, I straightened the story with Vitali on the way up, deciding that he had "died under interrogation." There was no point making an enemy out of a powerful man.

Aside from the debrief, there was nothing else to do, so most of us caught up on our sleep. Barlow informed us that the intel on the base was being acted on and a raid was being planned to neutralise it. As for the situation at the Complex and Hub, everyone was tight lipped so I figured it wasn't good news. I made enquiries about any evacuees coming up but no one was telling me anything.

Two days later, we were sat around chatting in a rec room when Schrader showed up, grinning like an idiot.

"What's up with you?" I asked. "Where have you been?"

"Never mind," he replied. "You'll see."

I wasn't in the mood for riddles but I let it slide. Especially as at that moment, Mir and Abomo appeared, closely followed by Kaur. She gave hugs all round, then, even better, pulled out some purloined Navy hooch from her backpack. She filled us in on what had been going on upstairs, starting with the prisoner transfer.

"We took delivery of Navarro okay, then that frog looking guy turned up with a couple of heavies in tow. He insisted the prisoner be transferred to his charge. He had all the paperwork, Skip. There was nothing I could do."

I shook my head, adding this to my list of issues to raise with Carswell. Kaur also gave us the sad news that Haugen hadn't made it. She'd heard he had been brought aboard but he'd died before she got the chance to see him.

That levelled the mood again, even more so when I

told Kaur about Pops and what had happened. She took it bad, needing a few minutes to herself and I kicked myself for not having seen what had been going on between them. Not that it would have changed anything, I suppose but it made his actions more puzzling to me.

Pouring the hooch, we took time to make a toast to absent friends. A few minutes later, Barlow returned to let us know of latest developments.

"There's a courier vessel just docked, ready to take your man here back to your CO." he tilted his head towards Kuruk. "This ship is staying in orbit for another few days before heading out to the nearest SWS. It may then be another day or so before you can get a ship home from there."

"Guess I'll join you then, Kuruk" I said. I knew Carswell would be keen to see us both. I turned to Barlow. "Can you arrange berth for the two of us on the courier ship?"

Barlow nodded, then turned as a familiar voice from the doorway commanded, "Belay that order!"
Yao strode in, bandaged and magnificent.

"What the – how?" I stuttered.

"You can thank your pilot." Yao's grin matched Schrader's.

"While you lot were lazing around up here, he made

four runs back down to the surface to help with evac from the Complex. He scooped me up on the last run. We were pretty much the last unit out."

Schrader shrugged. "I had to leave one lady behind, Skip. Didn't seem right to leave this one as well."

I could only grin in reply, then Yao barked out,

"So, Mr Obs, let your 2IC here get on the courier. You, sir are staying on board this ship – that's an order!"

Kaur smiled and said quietly to me, "You stay, Mike, I'll go with Kuruk. I'll tell Carswell you've been unavoidably delayed."

I considered the options. A slightly cramped journey with Kuruk to see an irate Carswell ... versus a few days in my pleasant, if still slightly cramped, cabin with Yao. I snapped off my sharpest salute and, with an "Aye ma'am!" grabbed a flask of hooch off the table, hooked my arm in Yao's and made for the door.

What could I say? Sometimes you just have to follow orders.

TO BE CONTINUED!

If you have enjoyed this book,
please leave a review on
Amazon. Thanks!

www.innsmouthgold.com

ABOUT THE AUTHOR

Robert Poyton is the founder of Innsmouth Gold.
Originally set up to provide an outlet for his Lovecraftian
musical projects, he also began writing fiction for IG,
starting with *Remnants*, a collection of ghost stories set
in the East Anglia Fens.

Robert grew up in the Golden Age of Marvel Comics,
Airfix kits, wargaming and Sven Hassel paperbacks. He
is a long-time fan of weird fiction, sword and sorcery and
science fiction books and movies.

Robert is a professional musician, currently heading
garage-horror band The Phobias.
He is also an experienced martial arts instructor,
having published a number of instructional books
and training films on Chinese and Russian arts.

Born and raised in East London, Robert now lives in
rural Bedfordshire, where he enjoys making a noise
and swinging sharp objects around.

www.wardroberecords.com
www.systemauk.com

THE DUNWICH TRILOGY

FAST PACED MODERN MYTHOS ACTION!

Based around the crumbling seaport on England's desolate East Coast, this modern take on Lovecraft's classic *The Dunwich Horror* sees unsuspecting people wrestling with the horrors of the Cthulhu Mythos!

THE DUNWICH NIGHTMARE

DC Marcus Hinds and journalist Suzy Bainbridge are drawn into a mystery following a series of grisly murders at Dunwich. Could there be a connection to the nearby top secret government research facility?

THE DUNWICH CRISIS

The scale of the conspiracy is revealed as Marcus and Suzy are pulled deeper into the nightmare. Meanwhile an ancient evil stirs in the depths of the North Sea and the world is about to change forever!

THE DUNWICH LEGACY

The true purpose of the CERN network is revealed. Marcus and Suzy plunge into the *world beyond,* as two ancient forces fight for the future of the planet.

ASSAULT TEAM 5
VOLUME TWO
HUNTED!

Following their return from the Copernicus 9 mission, Naylor and the team are drawn deeper into the political crisis on Earth. Meanwhile, the possibility of an internal leak puts the whole unit on edge.

When AT5 are tasked to find and retrieve a rogue corporate chemist, thinks quickly go wrong. Stranded on a desert planet, the team find themselves up against not only the Cartel, but also a crack mercenary team… and the hunters become the hunted!

OUT NOW!
In paperback or PDF download.
Available via Amazon or direct from
www.innsmouthgold,.com

DARE YOU UNCOVER THE SECRETS OF INNSMOUTH?

INNSMOUTH!

Decaying New England seaport, creation of iconic weird tale author HP Lovecraft.

But what if it were a real place? What if ripples from that accursed town were to spread out across the world?

Inspired by family documents and photos, this collection brings together tales and poems reflecting the legacy of Innsmouth throughout the ages.

From the loss of King John's treasure in the Wash, to the truth behind Britain's largest earthquake.

From secret U-boat missions to the Summer of Love. From yuppie developers to urban explorers. And from the sultry Pacific to the frozen Antarctic. No one who comes into contact with *Innsmouth Echoes* survives unchanged.

Because Innsmouth is not just a place... it's a state of mind.

THE WOLF WHO WOULD BE KING

A dynamic new Sword and Sorcery series in the spirit of Robert E. Howard!

WOLF IN SHADOWS

The saga begins! The tale of a Northern youth's first encounter with the ancient civilisation of Adelphis. Of the danger and intrigue that lurks below the sophisticated veneer. Of the perils of unholy sorcery. And of how a lone wolf becomes leader of the biggest pack of thieves in the city.

WOLF IN CHAINS

The young barbarian settles into his role as Royal Bodyguard. But a diplomatic mission to the desert city of Sahkmet plunges him into fresh intrigue – and the Wolf is chained! Meanwhile, an undead sorcerer is uniting the Desert Hordes and leading them on a merciless crusade. Can a northern barbarian hold the key to defeating this ancient evil?

WOLF IN THE NORTH

Tired of the intrigues of the south, Llorc returns to his homeland. He finds a country beset by strife. For a fearsome berserker has seized the Iron Crown and the Eight Clans stand poised on the brink of civil war. Llorc must guide a group of refugees through an increasingly hostile land, where ancient legends come to life. He may even have to face the gods themselves to save his people!

ANCESTORS AND DESCENDANTS

Ancestors - we all have them.
Family lines that extend deep
into the past and, sometimes,
into the future.

The works of HP Lovecraft
are full of references
to twisted family trees, evil
ancestors, and degenerate
descendants. Inheritance
and legacy, rebirth and
decay. This anthology
explores both prequels and
sequels to Lovecraftian tales.

Seventeen stories that tell of the descendants of
Randolph Carter and the aftermath of the fateful
1928 Innsmouth raid.

You will discover the dark history of the de la Poers,
read of the early days of the artist Pickman, and learn
the secrets of Erich Zann.

From downtown Arkham to distant Venus, from the dawn
of time to the far flung future; this unique collection, by
authors old and new, seeks to expand and explore the rich
Mythos legacy left to us by the Father of the Weird Tale.

OUT NOW!
In paperback or PDF download.
Available via Amazon or direct from
www.innsmouthgold,.com